No!

She was his target, for God's sake! A possible traitor, intending to sell data that could do irreparable harm to her country. He'd played this game once, had ignored his instincts and fallen for a woman who'd damned near killed him—literally. It had taken long, painful months to recover from that fiasco.

Problem was, his instincts worked against his intellect this time. Common sense said to back off, but his gut said Mallory Dawes had no knowledge of the disk planted in her suitcase.

Cutter went with his gut.

Bending, he covered her mouth with his.

Dear Reader,

When I was a kid, my dad was stationed for three years at a U.S. Air Force base northeast of Paris. During those exciting years, I developed a love of all things French. One of my greatest joys has been sharing that love with my husband. One trip in particular stands out in our memory.

We were meandering through Normandy, touring the D-Day beaches, sampling goat cheese, enjoying the local wine, and suddenly, there it was! Magical, mystical Mont St. Michel. I still get a catch in my throat when I remember our first glimpse of those medieval walls surmounted by the incredible cathedral. And I always wonder what the heck that driver was doing when the tide came in and floated his bus out to sea.

I didn't know then I was going to be a romance writer. Now that I am, it's great fun to share some of our world travels. Hope you enjoy!

Merline Lovelace

Merline Lovelace

STRANDED WITH A SPY

Silhouette®

Romantic

SUSPENSE

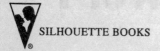

SILHOUETTE BOOKS

ISBN-13: 978-0-373-27553-3
ISBN-10: 0-373-27553-6

STRANDED WITH A SPY

Books by Merline Lovelace

Silhouette Romantic Suspense

MERLINE LOVELACE

An Air Force brat, Merline Lovelace grew up on military bases all around the world. She spent twenty-three years in the United States Air Force herself, pulling tours in Taiwan, Vietnam and at the Pentagon before she hung up her uniform for good and decided to try her hand at writing. She now has more than sixty-five published novels under her belt, with more than nine million copies of her works in print.

Merline and her own handsome hero live in Oklahoma. When she's not glued to her keyboard, she loves traveling to exotic locations, chasing little white balls around the golf course and enjoying long, lazy dinners with family and friends. Be sure to check www.merlinelovelace.com for release dates of future books.

To my darling, who loves to ramble and explore as much as I do. Thanks for the castles of the Loire Valley, picnicking under the arches of the Pont du Gard, lunch at the Ritz Carlton in Cannes and most of all— for Mont St. Michel.

Prologue

With the threat of bombs being detonated in midair by fanatics heavy in their minds, the inspectors screening the baggage going aboard the nonstop flight from D.C.'s Dulles Airport to Paris took no chances.

Bomb dogs sniffed long rows of suitcases and other checked items before handlers slung the pieces onto the conveyor for X-ray screening. Additional handlers waited down line to remove the items from the conveyor and load them onto carts for transport to the Boeing 777 parked out on the ramp.

Certain pieces received additional scrutiny before hitting the cart. Specially trained inspectors pulled

off luggage electronically tagged by ticket agents as
having been checked by individuals who fit certain
profiles, who looked nervous or whose body language
was in some way suspicious. Each of these bags were
opened and their contents closely examined.

The inspector pawing through one of those bags
had worked security at the General Services Administration Headquarters before transferring to the
Transportation Security Agency. Otherwise he might
not have recognized the logo on the computer disk
he found tucked inside a commercial CD case.

"Hey, Chief!"

The call jerked his supervisor's head around.
"What have you got?"

"The case says it's a CD by a blues singer by the
name of Corinne Bailey Rae, but the disk has no
markings except this."

He pointed to a tiny blue square on the inner rim
of the silver disk. Inside the square were the letters
GSA, with a small star forming the crossbar of the *A.*

"That's the General Services Administration logo.
The disk is government property."

"Wouldn't be the first time a civil servant ripped
off government supplies for private use," his supervisor mused, "but let's see what's on it."

Careful to handle the disk by the rim with his
gloved hands, the inspector slipped it into the
computer at his boss's workstation and clicked on the

single file that popped up. Seconds later the computer screen painted with line after line of names, addresses, birthdays and other identifying data.

Several names were highlighted in bold print. The one halfway down the first page elicited a startled *"Sonuvabitch"* from the inspector and drained all color from his supervisor's face.

Grabbing his phone, the supervisor punched a speed-dial number that connected him directly with the TSA Operations Center.

"This is Peterson. I've got a Code One!"

Chapter 1

A crisp September breeze rustled the leaves of the chestnut trees lining a quiet side street just off Massachusetts Avenue, in the heart of Washington, D.C.'s embassy district. When a taxi pulled up at an elegant townhouse halfway down the block, the driver frowned and shot a quick look in the rearview mirror.

"You sure you got the right address?"

"I'm sure." His passenger peeled off two bills. "Keep the change."

Despite the hefty tip, the driver's frown stayed in place as his fare hauled his beat-up leather carryall out of the cab.

No big surprise there, Cutter Smith thought sardonically. He hadn't slept in going on forty-eight hours and he hadn't shaved in twice that long. And not even four days' worth of raspy whiskers could disguise the scars on the right side of his chin and neck. When most people noticed the puckered skin, they quickly turned away. Others, like the cabbie, looked long and hard, as if memorizing the face that went with the scars in case they later had to pick him out of a police lineup.

As Cutter hefted his carryall and mounted the front steps, his gaze went to the discreet bronze plaque beside the door. The carefully polished lettering identified the townhouse as home to the offices of the Special Envoy to the President of the United States. Most Washingtonians familiar with the political spoils system knew the position of Special Envoy was one of those meaningless jobs handed out to wealthy campaign contributors with a yen for a fancy title and a Washington office. Only a very small, very select circle knew the Special Envoy also served as head of OMEGA, an agency so secret that its operatives were activated only in extreme situations.

Or, as in Cutter's case, reactivated. He'd returned from a month-long undercover operation in Central America only this morning, had conducted an exhaustive debrief and was headed home when a call from OMEGA control had turned him around.

Wondering what the hell was so urgent, he reached for the brass latch on the red-lacquered door. He knew it had to be something big for his boss to direct him to enter via the townhouse's front door instead of going through the labyrinthine maze that led from the secret entrance in an underground parking lot a half block away.

The receptionist who buzzed him in knew him by sight but still carefully checked his ID before passing him into the area ruled by the Special Envoy's executive assistant. The ornate Louis XV desk was normally occupied by Elizabeth Wells, a serene, silver-haired grandmother who regularly qualified at the expert level on the 9mm Sig Sauer nestled in a handy compartment in her desk.

But Elizabeth had fallen while doing a foxtrot with her latest beau on a Big Band Potomac Cruise. While she recovered from hip replacement surgery, a temp was handling her duties. An *extremely* well-qualified temp, with the necessary top-level security clearances, background and smarts to handle Elizabeth's extraordinarily sensitive duties.

Gillian Ridgeway was the daughter of two of OMEGA's most legendary operatives. She was also goddaughter to the man she referred to as Uncle Nick, OMEGA's current director. As luck would have it, she happened to be home on leave from her job at the American Embassy in Beijing when Elizabeth hit the deck. Nick Jensen had jumped on Gillian's offer to fill in for his temporarily disabled assistant.

Tall and slender, Gillian had inherited her mother's ready smile and her father's black hair and startlingly blue eyes. The twenty-six-year-old already had half the male operatives seriously in lust. That she'd also won the friendship and respect of OMEGA's female agents was testimony to her bright, engaging personality.

"Hi, Jilly." Depositing his carryall beside a leafy palm, Cutter crossed the parquet floor. "What's up?"

"Uncle Nick will explain all, Slash."

Gillian had assumed Cutter's code designation was a play on his first name. He hadn't disabused her.

"Go on in. He's waiting for you."

Nick Jensen, code name Lightning, didn't look like anyone's uncle, honorary or otherwise, when Cutter entered his office. Nor did he look like the owner of a string of outrageously expensive watering holes that catered to the rich and famous. He looked, Cutter thought with a lift of one brow, ready to chew nails and spit them out like shrapnel.

"Sorry, Slash." His jaw tight, Nick yanked at his Italian silk tie and popped the top button of his white shirt. "I know you haven't even changed your watch from jungle time yet, but I need to send you back into the field."

"No problem. What's the op?"

"I think we might finally have a lead on the Russian."

Cutter's pulse kicked up a half dozen notches. OMEGA had been trying to nail the shadowy figure known only as the Russian for more than a year.

"Mike Callahan will act as your controller." Nick shot back his cuff to check the sleek Swiss job on his wrist. "He's choppering up from Quantico. Should be about fifteen minutes out."

Cutter nodded, considerably reassured by the information. Whatever this mission entailed, it would go down a hell of a lot smoother with Mike Callahan, code name Hawkeye, handling things on this end. A former military cop, Hawk was a cool head and a dead shot.

"In the meantime," Nick said grimly, "we've got two hundred and thirty passengers cooling their heels at Dulles while maintenance works a small 'mechanical' problem on their aircraft. We suspect one of those passengers is on her way to connect with the Russian."

He slapped a file down on a mahogany conference table the size of a soccer field. Pinned to the front of the folder was a color photo of a tight-lipped blonde with most of her face hidden behind oversized sunglasses.

"A looker," Cutter commented, "but obviously not happy with the world. Who is she?"

"Mallory Dawes."

Nick said the name as if Cutter should know it, then gave an impatient shake of his head.

"Sorry. I forgot the crap hit the fan after you left for Central America. Dawes is…or was, until a few days ago…a staffer for Congressman Ashton Kent, Chairman of the House Banking and Trade Committee."

"The old goat knows how to pick 'em," Cutter commented, taking in the chiseled cheekbones and chin-length sweep of pale-gold hair.

"As a matter of fact, that's precisely what Dawes claimed in the sexual harassment complaint she filed. Said Kent admitted hiring the males in his office based on their brains and the females on their bra size. The comment came right after he reportedly groped her a second time and she allegedly whacked him with a copy of the *Congressional Record.*"

"Reportedly. Allegedly. I'm getting the impression Dawes's complaint boiled down to a case of she said/he said."

"It did. An investigator dismissed it two days ago for lack of evidence, but the media had a field day with the charge."

Cutter eyed the angry blonde again. "Bet they made her life hell in the process."

"And then some. We suspect that may be why Dawes quit her job, cleaned out her desk and departed the House of Representatives with a disk containing the names, addresses, social security numbers and bank account numbers of more than twenty million government employees. Including," Nick drawled, "the President of the United States."

Cutter whistled, low and long. That explained the high pucker factor. All brisk business now, Nick filled him in on the background.

"Kent's Committee recently conducted a series of closed hearings on the vulnerability of U.S. banks to hacking. One of the witnesses demonstrated just how easy it was to obtain this kind of sensitive data. We suspect Dawes secretly made a copy of the information this guy extracted from various sources before the file was destroyed."

"And we think she plans to sell the data?"

"We think that's a distinct possibility. Mallory Dawes isn't a happy camper right now. After the arbitrator dismissed her claim, she spoke on camera. The woman sounded both bruised and angry. Talked about how the accuser had become the accused, and how she wasn't given the protection she was supposed to be afforded under the law. What better way to get back at the system that failed you than by selling personal data to the highest black-market bidder?"

"Which would most likely be the Russian," Cutter acknowledged grimly.

OMEGA suspected the nameless, faceless thug had masterminded at least two other massive identity thefts. Both had wreaked havoc on the international financial scene and had devastating effects on the lives of millions of individuals. One of those individuals had been Cutter's great-aunt May, who'd lost her entire life savings in a series of swift, incredibly complex and as yet untraceable wire transfers.

Cutter *really* wanted to nail this bastard.

"Do we have a specific link between Dawes and the Russian?"

"Intelligence picked up an e-mail indicating he expects a major delivery soon."

No small feat, both men knew, given the billions of electronic communications screened daily.

"We also have evidence suggesting he's on the move. Intel thinks he may be headed for Paris."

"Like our girl, Dawes," Cutter said softly.

"Exactly."

"We've got her under close surveillance at Dulles while we substitute a disk containing fake data for the one in her bag. We're also tagging the CD's case with a monitoring device so we can track its every move. I want you in Paris, waiting at the airport, when she and the bag come off the plane. With any luck, she'll lead you to the Russian."

Lightning checked his watch again.

"We have an air force jet standing by at Andrews. The chopper that delivers Mike will take you out to the base. You've got fifteen minutes to shower, shave and jump into clean clothes. Field Dress has every-

thing you need upstairs. Mac's working your comm
as we speak. Your cover is businessman on vacation."

At his operative's pained look, Lightning relaxed
into a smile for the first time since the call had come
from the White House less than a half hour ago. A
former Army Ranger, Cutter still preferred boots and
floppy-brimmed boonie hats to business suits.

"Sorry, Slash. It was the best Field Dress could do
on short notice. Take the file on Dawes with you and
read it on the chopper."

"Will do."

Cutter climbed aboard the chopper less than
twenty minutes later. His hair was still damp from his
ninety-second shower and his cheeks stung from the
aftershave he'd splashed on after scraping off his
whiskers. His boots and jeans were gone, traded for
a suede sport coat and open-necked white shirt paired
with black slacks and polished loafers.

Shutting out the whap-whap of the chopper's
rotors, he slid the folder from the expensive
Moroccan leather briefcase Field Dress had thrust at
him on his way out the door and settled in to read the
background dossier on Mallory Dawes.

Mallory sat quietly in a corner of the International
Waiting Area. She'd had to slip out the back door of
her apartment to evade the reporters camped out

front. With escape so close, the last thing she wanted now was to draw attention to herself.

Shielded behind tinted glasses, her gaze roamed her increasingly impatient fellow passengers. Some paced, some checked the monitors for an update on their departure time, others flipped through magazines. A young mother kept twin toddlers on security leashes and walked them like frisky puppies, hoping to use up their store of energy. She'd taken a nearby seat a while ago and tried to strike up a conversation. Mallory had cut her off with the excuse of having to go to the ladies' room.

The past weeks had taught her to distrust *everyone*. Reporters had resorted to all kinds of ruses in their relentless pursuit of intimate details about her life and loves. One had disguised himself as a deliveryman and shown up at Mallory's apartment with a dozen roses. Others had donned overalls and sifted through the Dumpster behind her apartment. As voracious as scavengers feeding on rotting corpses, they'd dug up skeletons Mallory didn't know she had.

Like the junior-high-school "sweetheart" who couldn't wait to tell the world how hot she was. As best she could recall, she'd kissed the kid once, while playing spin the bottle at some eighth- or ninth-grade party.

Then there was the lobbyist she'd dated all of twice, yet he claimed they'd had a torrid affair after she picked him up in a bar. It was a *sushi* bar, for God's sake, and *he'd* picked her up, but that hadn't made for good copy. Her mouth twisting, Mallory folded her arms and stared out the plate-glass windows until an announcement came over the speakers.

"We apologize for the delay, ladies and gentlemen. Our minor maintenance issue has been resolved. Flight 17 nonstop to Charles De Gaulle Airport, Paris, is now ready for boarding."

Thank God!

Because of tightened security on international flights, Mallory had checked everything but a small wallet purse containing her passport, ID and the one credit card she hadn't maxed out. She'd drawn against the others for loans to pay the lawyers she'd had to hire to defend herself against Congressman Kent's counter-allegations.

Don't think about the legal bills waiting to be paid, she lectured herself sternly as she boarded the transport that would take the passengers out to the aircraft. Don't think about the ugliness or smut or vicious lies.

Think about France. Undulating vineyards. Fairytale castles. Crusty bread and melt-in-your-mouth pastries.

And anonymity. Blessed anonymity.

Ten whole days with no reporters hounding her, no microphones shoved in her face. She'd lose herself on back roads. Put the awful mess behind her.

Nine hours, she thought as she found her seat and buckled in. Nine hours flying through the night, then freedom.

As soon as the jumbo jet reached cruising altitude, she plugged in her earphones, slipped on the eye mask provided by the airline and reclined her seat.

Ms. Dawes was one cool customer, Cutter decided, watching from a few feet away at the baggage carousel.

He'd tracked her from the moment she exited the aircraft. She'd looked straight ahead as she stood in line at passport control, didn't so much as nod or speak to any of her fellow passengers. Same here at the baggage carousel. Below the shield of her sunglasses, her mouth was set in a line that warned off all comers.

With seeming nonchalance, Cutter pulled out a slim cell phone. Mackenzie Blair, Nick's wife and OMEGA's guru of all things electronic, had packed the slim case with enough gadgetry and software to make Bill Gates drool.

She'd replaced the built-in camera with one so powerful she swore it would capture a mosquito in flight a block away. With a flick of one button, Cutter could reverse the lens and activate an iris scanner. The digitized image identified him instantaneously to his controller at OMEGA headquarters. Voice-recognition software provided additional security, as did the satellite encryption transmissions. Not even the spooks at the National Intelligence Collection and Processing Center could intercept these calls.

What interested Cutter most at the moment was the embedded GPS transceiver that caused the phone to vibrate when the compact disk tucked into Mallory Dawes's suitcase moved so much as an inch.

It was moving now. The vibrations tickled Cutter's palm and had every one of his nerves jumping in response. Screwing in an earpiece, he flipped up the phone and made like the other half dozen or so passengers busy calling home or confirming reservations now that they'd landed.

"I've got movement."

He didn't bother to identify himself. The phone took care of that. Mike Callahan's reply came through the earpiece.

"Roger that, Slash. I'm tracking the case via the airport's security cameras. It's on a baggage cart, headed your way."

Cutter acknowledged the transmission and tucked the phone back in his pocket. As the vibrations grew stronger, his instincts went on full alert.

His gut told him the most likely spot for the Russian or one of his cohorts to make the pickup was right here at the airport. Odds were it would happen shortly after Dawes claimed her bag.

He was right on her tail when she exited through passport control, had the woman and her roller bag firmly in his sights when she strode through the terminal, felt the phone vibrating like hell in his shirt pocket as she marched up to a rental-car counter.

It was still vibrating when he tossed his briefcase and carryall in a rental car some minutes later and trailed her midget Peugeot out of Charles De Gaulle Airport.

Chapter 2

Mallory was amazed that she could still function with semiefficiency.

The long flight across the Atlantic should have wiped her out, especially coming on top of all the weeks of stress. Not to mention the sleepless nights wondering why she hadn't just quit after Congressman Kent had grabbed her ass the first time.

Dillon Porter, Kent's senior staffer and Mallory's closest friend on the Hill, had smoothed things over that first time. Dillon had agreed with her that their boss was a throwback, a total Neanderthal. He'd also warned that Kent was so slick, any charges Mallory brought against him would slide off his Teflon-coated back.

How right Dillon had been!

Only now, after two hours of ambling west along the two-lane road that led from Paris to Evreux, were Mallory's jagged nerves beginning to smooth out. The brisk sea breeze as she neared the coast of Normandy blew through the open windows of her pint-sized rental like the breath of life.

This wasn't the route she'd laid out when she'd planned this long-dreamed-of vacation in such meticulous detail. A history major in college, she'd intended to spend at least three days exploring Paris before heading south to visit the medieval walled city of Carcassonne and the Roman ruins at Nîmes.

With the miasma of the hearing hanging over her, however, Mallory had decided to reverse her itinerary. She needed calm and space and solitude, which she certainly wouldn't get in the bustle of Paris. She'd hit the city on her way back. Maybe. For now she'd just follow the coast and let the winds blow away the stink of the past weeks.

Her first stop was Caen, William the Conqueror's stronghold and the site of vicious battles during the Second World War invasion of Normandy. Mallory squeezed out of her rental car and treated herself to a flaky quiche and a sinfully rich napoleon eaten at an outdoor café in the shadow of the castle walls. After lunch she visited the museum housing the Bayeux Tapestry embroidered by William's wife, Matilda, after her husband had conquered England.

Musing at the vagaries of fate that had one nation invading another, only to be invaded itself centuries later by the nation it had once conquered, Mallory drank in the history that went into the hundred-and-sixty-eight-foot tapestry. The segment that dealt with William's visit to a nearby holy place spawned another spur-of-the-moment decision.

"Mont St. Michel," she murmured, her gaze fixed on the embroidered panel depicting mounted warriors pulling pilgrims from the treacherous waters surrounding the shrine. Mesmerized by the scene, she consulted her plastic-coated, foldaway tourist map.

The shrine was only a little over an hour from Caen. Not on her original route, but so what? She wasn't too jet-lagged yet. She could do another hour of driving easy. After she'd explored the ancient abbey, she'd find a nice little seaside pension and crash.

Bad decision, Mallory thought two and a half hours later.

Very bad.

The countryside of Lower Normandy was pretty enough. She'd left the sea behind at Caen to cut across a broad peninsula dotted with magnificent forests and tranquil streams flowing through rich farmlands. Apple orchards lined the road and hand-painted signs pointed to tasting stands for Camembert, Livarot and Pont l'Evêque cheese. Without intending to, Mallory had stumbled onto France's Wine and Cheese Road.

Which would have been fine except that the fall harvest was in full swing. Tractors hauling trailers mounded with apples competed for road space with busloads of tourists come to sample fresh-squeezed cider and pungent cheese. As Mallory inched through a picturesque village behind yet another tractor, she looked in vain for an inn or a pension. She was ready to call it a day *and* a night.

The tractor finally turned off at a crossroads. A tilted signpost pointed to villages with names Mallory couldn't pronounce. Below the signpost was a blue historical sign indicating that Mont St. Michel was five kilometers away.

"Finally!"

Surely there would be plenty of hotels at such a touristy spot. Aiming her tiny rental car in the direction of the sea once more, she soon left the forests and orchards behind. The topography flattened to marshy fields topped by feathery grass. The tangy scent of the ocean again flavored the air.

Then Mallory turned a bend in the road and there it was, rising out of the salt marsh. Stunned, she

pulled to the side of the road and sat there, arms
looped over the wheel.

Mont St. Michel was a small island, an outcrop-
ping of solid granite thrusting up from sand flats at
the mouth of St. Malo Bay. A defensive wall bristling
with turrets and a fourteenth-century barbican encir-
cled the rock at its base. Above the battlements, a
village of slate-roofed buildings stair-stepped up the
steep slopes. A magnificent twelfth-century abbey
crowned the island, overwhelming in its size, over-
powering in its grandeur. Atop the abbey's tall spire
was a gilded statue of Saint Michael that glinted in
the afternoon sun.

According to Mallory's guidebook, the Archangel
Michael had appeared on this spot in 708 AD. The
glorious abbey was built to honor that visitation. All
through the Middle Ages, pilgrims had risked the
treacherous tides that rushed in, cutting the island off
from the mainland, to worship at the site. Modern-
day tourists were no less enthralled. Mesmerized by
the magnificent sight, Mallory paid no attention to the
tour bus that chugged by her, spewing diesel exhaust.

The driver of the vehicle some yards behind the
lumbering bus cursed as he approached the car pulled
onto the side of the road. Cutter had been swallowing
exhaust for twenty minutes. He'd had to, to keep some
distance between him and his target. God knew there
wasn't any other cover on this stretch of flat salty marsh.

Now he had no choice but to drive right past the woman and onto the causeway leading to the island dead ahead. The causeway was elevated above the sand flats and wide enough to accommodate dozens of parked cars and buses. Cutter could turn around easily enough if the woman he was tailing didn't follow him onto the bridge.

"Come on, Dawes," he muttered, "put it in gear."

He kept her in the rearview mirror and was all set to make a turn when the cell phone in his pocket began to vibrate. The car behind him eased back onto the road.

"That's right. Come to Papa."

Dividing his attention between the vehicle behind and the battlements now looming before him, Cutter cruised the long bridge. The tide was out, baring the hard-packed sand below. Overflow traffic was being directed to park on the sand, but a minivan pulled out of a parking space atop the causeway as Cutter got close. Whipping into the space, he remained in his vehicle with the engine idling while his target neared the island.

He speared a quick glance at the walls looming above him. Was this where Dawes planned to make contact with the Russian or one of his henchmen? Or would she just diddle away a few hours, as she had in Caen? Or had she tipped to the fact that she was being followed and had decided to lead her tail away from a possible rendezvous point instead of toward it?

Cutter was ninety-nine-percent certain that wasn't the case. With the directional signal implanted in her suitcase to guide him, he'd stayed well out of her line of sight while on the road. He'd mounted a closer surveillance in Caen, waiting, watching, his instincts on full alert. But she hadn't removed the disk from the suitcase locked in the trunk of her rental car. He'd trailed her into the museum, keeping well back, knowing the signal device would alert him if someone *else* retrieved it. No one had.

Wondering if this pile of rock would be the rendezvous point, Cutter narrowed his eyes behind his aviator sunglasses and watched as Dawes drove along the causeway. The bridge was a quarter-mile long and raised some ten or twelve feet above the sand flats. Dawes drove the length of the causeway, searching for a parking space, before nosing down a ramp to the hard-packed sand.

When she exited her rental, Cutter held his breath. Would she unlock the trunk? Slip the disk into the wallet-type purse slung over her shoulder?

To his intense disappointment, she did neither. Instead she joined a throng of tourists decamping from a bus and trekked up the ramp toward the barbican. Muttering a curse, Cutter pulled out his cell phone.

"The target has exited her vehicle," he advised Mike Callahan after the iris scan and voice data print had verified his identity. "Again."

"Roger that. You want to confirm the location? GPS is showing her parked about ten yards off the causeway leading to the island of Mont St. Michel, in what should be about eight feet of water."

"The tide's out, Hawkeye, so it's high and dry. She's walking up to the island from her car, minus her suitcase."

"Could be intending to establish initial contact before making the drop."

"Could be," Cutter agreed, shouldering open his car door. "Check the tide tables for me, will you? I want to know how long we've got here."

"Will do."

He could have spared Mike the trouble, Cutter realized as he trailed his target toward the massive gates guarding the entrance to the walled town. Warning signs posted at several points along the causeway warned visitors in five different languages to stick to designated walkways to avoid dangerous quicksand. The signs also advised that high tide would occur at eighteen hundred hours that evening.

Three and a half hours, Cutter thought grimly. Plenty of time for Ms. Dawes to establish contact, return to her car and retrieve the disk.

As he had at Caen, he stayed out of her line of sight. Not hard to do, with so many tourists thronging the narrow, cobbled streets. Then again, Dawes made for an easy tail. She wasn't all that tall. Five-six, according to the background dossier OMEGA had hastily compiled on her. Yet her cap of shining blond hair acted like a beacon amid the shadows thrown by the tall, narrow buildings lining the streets and alleys. The navy blazer she wore with a white tank top and jeans also stood out among the post-summer throng of primarily middle-aged tourists in jogging suits and windbreakers.

Eyeing the trim rear and slender thighs encased by those jeans, Cutter had to admire Congressman Kent's taste, if not his morals. Ms. Dawes's behind looked eminently gropeable. Her front looked pretty good, too. Narrow waist. Full breasts. A determined chin softened by lips he suspected might tempt a man to sin if she ever smiled. Cutter could certainly understand why the clown she'd picked up in a D.C. bar had described her to the press as a real piece of eye candy.

But it was the way she moved that stirred unwelcome memories. Cutter had known a woman who walked with that same hip-swinging grace once. He still wore the scars she'd left on him.

Which was probably why he noticed when Ms. Dawes began to move with considerably less elegance. Obviously, the climb up the winding streets and steep stairs was taking its toll. Her pace got slower and more deliberate. Her shoulders started to sag. She paused more often to study shop windows displaying fresh pastries, cheeses, handmade lace and the inevitable cheap souvenirs.

Cutter was thirty yards behind her when she veered toward a small café carved out of the rock below the walls of the cathedral. Potted geraniums added splashes of color to the tiny patio, which contained all of three tables. Dawes dropped into a chair at the only empty table. When she shoved her sunglasses to the top of her head to study the menu, lines of exhaustion were etched into her face.

Cutter continued his surveillance from a combination *boulangerie* and sandwich shop across the street. Surrounded by the seductive aroma of fresh-baked baguettes and twisted loaves of rye, he ordered a ham and Swiss and coffee. He carried both to a stand-up table in the window and had the crusty sandwich halfway to his mouth when he froze.

Eyes narrowing to slits behind his mirrored sunglasses, Cutter assessed the heavyset male who scooted his chair around to face Dawes. Early fifties. Dressed as a tourist in no-press khaki knit pants, a blue windbreaker and a baseball cap with some kind of a logo on it. Heavy jowls, flushed cheeks and a knowing smile that lifted the hairs on the back of Cutter's neck.

The guy knew Dawes. He'd recognized her, perhaps had been waiting for her. Whipping out his cell phone, Cutter zoomed in on the man's red face and took several quick shots with the instrument's built-in, jazzed-up camera. A click of a button transmitted the photos instantly to OMEGA. Cutter followed with a terse instruction to Mike Callahan.

"Give me an ID on this guy, and fast."

"Will do."

He needed to get closer for the sensitive receiver built into the phone to pick up the conversation between his target and the fleshy tourist. Abandoning his coffee and sandwich, Cutter exited the *boulangerie* and crossed the cobbles. He kept to the shadows thrown by the cathedral directly above. With each step closer, the receiver filtered out the background noise from the busy street until Dawes's voice came through sharp and angry.

"No, thank you."

"Ahhh, c'mon. We're both 'Mericans. Let me buy you a glass of wine. Jes' one glass."

From the sound of it, the supposed tourist had already downed several glasses. Or wanted to give that impression.

"Didn't you hear me? I said no."

Dawes's icy reply didn't deter the man. His heavy cheeks creasing into a smirk, he hooked his arm over the back of her chair.

"I heard you. From what Congressman Kent and those others said, though, your 'no' really means 'maybe.'"

With a sound of disgust, Dawes slipped her sunglasses back onto her nose and gathered her purse.

"Hey! Where y'going?"

Stumbling to his feet, the big man tossed some bills down on his table and followed her into the street. If this was an act, Cutter thought, it was a damned good one.

Dawes kept her face averted and marched stiffly ahead, but that didn't deter the persistent tourist.

"The papers said you like to pick up men in bars," he said, loud enough to turn the heads of several passersby. "I've got a couple hours to kill before I have to climb back onto that damned bus. Plenty of time for us to have some fun."

Shoulders rigid, Dawes turned into a narrow alley to escape her tormentor. The tourist followed, with Cutter some yards behind. Ingrained habit had him doing an instinctive sweep for obstacles, hostiles and possible escape routes. There didn't appear to be many of the latter.

Tall buildings with carved lintels and slate roofs leaned in on both sides, cutting off the sunlight and almost obscuring the flowers that decorated doorways and windowsills. A stone horse trough was set dead center in the middle of the cobbles, testimony to Mont St. Michel's main means of transportation for centuries.

"Wait up, sweet thing!" Dodging the watering

trough, the tourist grabbed his quarry's arm. "We kin…"

"Let go of me!" A mass of seething fury, Dawes whirled around and yanked her arm free of his hold. "Touch me again, you obnoxious ass, and I swear I'll…"

"You'll what?" He waggled his brows in an exaggerated leer. "Charge me with sexual harassment, like you did Congressman Kent?"

"I'll do what I *should* have done to Kent," she ground out through clenched teeth, "and knee you in your nut-sized brain."

The threat didn't faze her tormentor. If anything, it seemed to add spice to his sport.

"Whoo-ee. Aren't you a feisty one? That guy you dated in school said you liked it raunchy, even rough sometimes. That's fine with me."

Cutter kept to the shadows. He'd prefer not to break cover or show himself to his target, but the situation was starting to get ugly.

A few yards away, Mallory had come to the same conclusion. She knew damned well all she had to do was scream. They were only a few yards off a main street crowded with tourists. One panicked shriek, one piercing cry, and a dozen people would charge to her rescue.

Then the police would arrive on the scene. She'd have to deal with their questions, their carefully blank faces when this loudmouthed fool ranted about how she'd led him on, like she had all the others back in the States.

Better to handle the situation herself, utilizing one of the more effective moves she'd learned in the self-defense class she'd taken when she first got to D.C. Before the heel of her hand could connect with the bridge of the beefy tourist's nose, however, he jerked backward. A startled Mallory watched him lift off his feet. A second later, he landed butt-first in the stone horse trough.

"What the hell…?"

Cursing, he struggled to lever himself out of the narrow trough. The man who'd put him there planted a hand on his head, pushing him down and under.

As her attacker gurgled and flailed his arms and legs, Mallory's surprise gave way to fierce delight. The dunking went on a little too long, however. She was about to issue a curt order not to drown the bastard when the man holding him under relented.

The jerk who'd accosted her came up sputtering and ready to fight. When he shook the water from his eyes and got a good look at the individual looming above him, however, he plopped back down into the water.

"Smart move," his chastiser said in a voice as deep as it was cool and steady. "I suggest you listen next time a lady says no."

"Yeah, yeah, okay."

When the stranger straightened and stepped out
of the shadows, Mallory registered short-cropped
brown hair, wide shoulders and a well-cut sports
jacket paired with an open-necked shirt. Then she
saw the scars puckering one side of his neck and
swallowed a gulp. No wonder the loudmouthed
tourist had planted his butt back into the water.

"You okay?" the newcomer asked.

"I'm fine." Rattled by the incident and pissed at
having the first day of her precious vacation tainted
by the ugliness she'd come here to escape, Mallory's
response was somewhat less than gracious. "Thanks."

Her tone implied she could have handled the situation herself. She reinforced that impression by
sweeping past both men. The one still standing said
nothing, but the waterlogged tourist made the
mistake of muttering aloud, "Bitch."

The vicious epithet was followed by a yelp and
another splash. Mallory didn't slow or bother to look
around. For all she cared, the scarred stranger could
drown the moron.

Chapter 3

Mallory had never climbed so many steps in her life!

The stairs leading to the abbey were carved into the granite. In some places they climbed straight up. In others, they followed a zigzag pattern that shortened the rise but doubled the distance required to travel. She stopped several times along the way to shake the kinks out of her calves and was huffing long before she reached the small terrace that faced the abbey's magnificent vaulted doors.

If the steep climb and the wind whipping off the Bay of St. Malo hadn't stolen Mallory's breath, the view would have done the trick. Waiting for her heart to stop hammering, she leaned her elbows on the terrace wall. Far below, mud-brown flats stretched all the way to the sea. A storm was forming far out on the bay. Thunderclouds had piled up, forming a dramatic vista and no doubt accounting for the wind that whipped Mallory's hair.

She was surprised to see people walking across the flats. Signs posted all around Mont St. Michel warned about the dangers of quicksand. They also posted the time of the incoming tide.

Frowning, Mallory glanced at her watch. She'd wasted too much time in the village. She'd have to hurry her tour of the abbey to get back down to the parking lot before the water nipped at the rental's tires.

Adjusting her sunglasses, she eased into the stream of tourists entering the cathedral. She'd already decided not to join one of the guided tours that took visitors through the adjacent Benedictine monastery. After the nasty incident in the village, she was in no mood for the company of others. Instead, she slipped through the cathedral's massive doors and was immediately swallowed by the vastness of its nave.

Like most European churches, this one was laid out in the shape of a cross. The long main transept ended in a curved apse that faced to the east and the rising sun that symbolized Christ. The shorter, north-south transept bisected the main vestibule at the choir and led to richly decorated chapels.

Three tiers of soaring granite arches, all intricately carved and decorated, supported the vaulted ceiling high above Mallory's head. *Unlike* so many other European cathedrals, however, this one was filled with light. Gloriously white and shimmering, it poured in through the tiered windows and added a luminescent sheen to the gray granite walls.

Guidebook in hand, Mallory took in the richness of the altar and choir before exploring the side chapels. The musky scent of incense lingered in the alcoves and mixed with the smoke from hundreds of flickering votives. She stood for long moments before a bank of votives dominated by a stained-glass window depicting Saint Michael slaying a dragon.

Part of her ached to drop a franc in the slot, light a candle and pray for the strength to forgive Congressman Kent and everyone in the media who'd slandered her. The rest of her was still too bruised and hurt. She wasn't ready to forgive or forget, and she figured God would recognize a fake prayer quick enough.

Sighing, Mallory followed the signs pointing to the stairs that wound down to the crypts. There were two of these subterranean chambers, one under the north transept, one under the south. The first was big and ornate and contained the sarcophagi of previous bishops and abbots. The second was much smaller and plainer. Barrel-vaulted and constructed with Romanesque simplicity, it had the dank smell of centuries long past.

There, in the south crypt dedicated to Saint Martin, Mallory founded a semblance of the serenity that had eluded her upstairs. It was so quiet in the crypt, and so empty. The only objects in the round-roofed chamber were a plain altar topped by a wrought-iron cross and a narrow wooden prayer bench set alongside one wall.

Mallory eased onto the bench and leaned her shoulders against the granite wall. A chill seeped through her navy blazer, but she barely noticed it.

Why *couldn't* she forgive and forget? Why had she let Congressman Kent destroy her pride along with her reputation?

Her friend, Dillon Porter, had tried to warn her. In his serious, no-nonsense way, Kent's senior staffer had reminded his coworker how Jennifer Flowers and Monica Lewinsky had become the butt of so many vicious jokes. Yet Mallory had plowed ahead, convinced she had right on her side.

Yeah, sure.

With another long sigh, she tilted her head against the granite and closed her eyes. Maybe if she just sat here a while, the utter calm of this place would leach into her troubled soul.

What the hell was she doing?

Cutter lounged against a stone pillar, pretending

interest in a brochure he'd picked up at the entrance to the abbey. The brochure happened to be in Japanese, a fact that had escaped his attention until he'd been forced to hide behind the damned thing for going on twenty minutes now.

Was she waiting for someone? The Russian? The obnoxious tourist?

Or had the woman fallen asleep? Sure looked like it from where Cutter stood.

Her head rested against the granite wall. Her lashes feathered her cheek. The arms she'd hooked around her waist had loosened and sagged into her lap.

She'd stirred, blinking owlishly when the muted sound of an announcement drifted down the stairs. They were too deep in the bowels of the church to distinguish the words, and she was too lethargic to do more than turn her head toward the distant sound. Moments later, her lids had dropped and she was breathing deeply again. This time a small smile played at the corners of her lips.

Sweet dreams, Dawes?

Thinking about all the goodies you'll buy when and if you sell the data you stole?

Frowning, Cutter shot a quick look at his watch. The warning signs posted around the island were vivid in his head when the cell phone in his pocket began to vibrate. This motion had a different pattern from that of the GPS tracker attached to the disk in Dawes's suitcase.

That was Mike Callahan signaling him. He must have IDed the fleshy tourist. Keeping the entrance to the small crypt in sight, Cutter retreated into the dim recesses of the subterranean vault and screwed the phone's earpiece into his ear. A click of the receive button brought Callahan's face up on the screen.

"What have you got?"

His voice carried no more than a few feet in the dank, gloomy stillness. Callahan's came through the earpiece clearly.

"Your friend is Robert Walters."

A photo of the paunchy tourist replaced Mike's face. This shot showed him in a business suit, smiling for the camera as he gestured toward a warehouse with a sign announcing Walters Products.

"Age," Hawkeye reported succinctly, "fifty-three. Born, Sterling, Indiana. One hitch in the Navy. Made three trips to the altar, the same number to divorce court. Owns a siding-and-storm-door installation company in Indiana. He and two buddies are on a tour of the Normandy beaches, sponsored by their local American Legion."

"Doesn't sound like the profile of someone with ties to an international thug like the Russian."

"Didn't to me, either," Hawkeye agreed, "until I dug into his financials and discovered our boy Walters is six months behind in alimony to wife number two *and* wife number three. He also owes a cool hundred thou to his bookie. Seems he has a weakness for the ponies."

"Interesting."

"Yeah, it is. I'm working authorization to run his cell, home and business phones. Will get back to you as soon as... Hang on!"

The terse admonition came at precisely the same instant the instrument in Cutter's hand began to vibrate to a different pattern. Smothering a curse, he recognized the signal before Mike's voice cut back through his earpiece.

"We've got movement on the disk, Slash."

"Yeah, I'm receiving the signal."

"Is the target back at her vehicle?"

"No."

She hadn't moved, dammit! Not so much as an inch. She still dozed on that bench. Or pretended to. The perfect decoy.

Swearing viciously under his breath, Cutter took the stairs from the crypt two at a time. Tourists sent him startled looks as he raced through the cathedral, his footsteps echoing on the granite blocks.

Dodging a group of Chinese visitors, he burst through the abbey doors onto the small terrace. The western side looked to the sea. The south edge, he saw when he pushed through a gawking, pointing crowd, looked down over the causeway and what *used* to be the overflow parking lot.

The sand flats on either side of the causeway were empty now except for a single tour bus with its wheels awash in seawater…and Dawes's rented Peugeot, floating on the tide. As Cutter watched, tight-jawed, the little car bobbed farther and farther from the causeway.

Loudspeakers blared, slicing through the tourists' excited babble. An urgent message was broadcast first in French, then English, then in Japanese.

"Attention! Attention! The driver of Tour Bus Number Fifty-Seven must return to his vehicle immediately! The storm at sea has created a severe riptide. Your bus will soon be afloat."

So that was the muffled announcement that had failed to penetrate to the subterranean crypts! The off-shore winds had churned up a vicious riptide and sent it rushing in, well ahead of the posted times for normal high water.

Drivers alerted by the announcements had managed to clear most of the vehicles parked on the sand. Only two hadn't been rescued—the heavy tour bus with gray-green water now swirling up to its fender skirts and Mallory Dawes's lightweight Peugeot, at present floating on the outgoing current.

"Omigod!"

The shriek came from directly behind Cutter. He edged to the side to make room for the woman who elbowed her way through the crowd.

"That's my car!"

Her dismay spiraled into panic. Cupping her hands to her mouth, Dawes screamed at the ant-like figures on the causeway far below.

"Hey! You down there! That's my car floating away! *Do* something!"

Even she could see it was too late for anyone to save the little car. The fast-moving tide had already carried the vehicle a good half mile and it was starting to take on water. As she watched, horrified, the little car tipped to one side, rolled over and went wheels up. Like a puppy begging to have its stomach tickled, it floated a few more yards before slowly sinking into the sea.

Utter silence gripped the crowd. Cutter could swear he almost heard the gurgle of the bubbles that rose to the surface as the mini disappeared.

Sympathetic clucking noises from several of the Japanese tourists broke the stillness. Their tour guide approached a shell-shocked Dawes.

"Your car, yes?"

"Yes," she whispered raggedly.

"You must tell them, at the visitors' center."

Dawes couldn't tear her gaze from the gray-green water. She kept staring at the spot where the Peugeot had disappeared. One white-knuckled hand gripped the other, as if she were praying that the statue of Saint Michael perched on the steeple above her head would command the seas to part and the car to miraculously reappear.

"You must tell them," the tour guide insisted. "At the visitors' center."

Cutter's mind had been racing since he'd first spotted the bobbing vehicle. Whatever else Dawes might have intended to do with the data disk, his gut told him this little drama hadn't figured into her plan. It hadn't figured into his, either, but he sure as hell wasn't going to pass up the opportunity that had just been handed to him on a big, golden platter.

"This hasn't been your day, has it?"

The comment jerked Dawes's head around. She'd whipped off the sunglasses she'd used as a shield up to now, so this was Cutter's first glimpse of her eyes. Caramel-brown and flecked with gold, they were flooded with dismay…until they dropped to the puckered skin below his chin. Then the emotions Cutter had seen too many times to count clicked across her face. Curiosity came first, followed quickly by embarrassment at being caught staring.

Apparently Dawes was made of tougher stuff than most. Either that, or she understood how it felt to be gaped at. She didn't color up and quickly look away. Instead, her gaze lifted to his.

"No," she admitted, raising a hand to hold back her wind-whipped hair, "it hasn't."

Cutter had grimaced when Field Dress had saddled him with this bland businessman's cover but decided it would work like a charm in this situation.

"Maybe I can help. I have some contacts who know this area."

Like Nick Jensen, aka Lightning, who'd grown up in the back alleys of Cannes before being brought to the States and adopted by one of OMEGA's top agents. Any strings Mike Callahan couldn't pull through official channels, Nick could through his own.

Mallory struggled to hold back her hair and the hot tears stinging her eyes. Any other woman in her situation would have jumped at the offer. Any woman, that is, who hadn't been savaged by the media and made into a walking bull's-eye for predatory males.

Granted, this one had already come to her aid once. Yet those cool gray eyes and powerful shoulders didn't exactly put him in the tame category. Then there were those scars…

"Do you always go around rescuing women?"

The question came out sounding more suspicious and hostile than Mallory had intended. He answered with a raised brow and a shrug.

"Only those who seem to need it. Obviously, you don't. My mistake." With a nod, he turned away. "Good luck salvaging your car."

God! That mess with Congressman Kent had

turned her into a real bitch! Disgusted with herself, Mallory stopped him with a brusque apology.

"I'm sorry. It's just… Well…"

She decided he didn't need to know the sordid details behind her recent distrust of all things male.

"I'm sorry," she said again. "I, uh, appreciate the way you handled that jerk down in the village and I'd welcome any help retrieving my car. My suitcase is in the trunk. *And* my passport," she remembered on a new wave of dismay. "And all my traveler's checks!"

Stunned all over again, Mallory spun around to stare at the spot where her rental had disappeared. The sea now completely covered the mud flats. Except for the causeway, the island was cut off from the mainland.

As it had been for hundreds of years, when pilgrims had dared the treacherous sands to buy indulgence for their sins. Mallory was in no condition to appreciate the irony.

"Do you think…?"

Gulping, she tried to swallow her panic. All she had with her was a single credit card and the few francs tucked in the purse slung over her shoulder. Like a fool, she hadn't even carried her receipt for the traveler's checks on her person. The past weeks had shaken her to her core, it was true, but that was no excuse for sheer stupidity!

"Do you think they can get my car back? Or at least retrieve my passport and traveler's checks?"

"Maybe. Depends on how strong the riptide is and how far it carries the vehicle."

She whirled again, grabbing at the fragile hope he'd offered until he gently shattered that.

"I suspect you aren't the first tourist to lose a car to the tides, so I'm guessing there are probably a number of salvage companies in the area. It'll take time to mount that kind of an operation, though, and some big bucks. You'd better check with the rental company to see what their insurance covers."

Mallory's stomach took another dive. She'd barely glanced at the half dozen or so insurance clauses she'd initialed when she'd rented the Peugeot. Now phrases like *negligence, collateral damage,* and *criminal acts* popped into her head.

Surely the rental company couldn't hold her responsible for the loss! Okay, there were signs posted all over Mont St. Michel. And yes, she'd heard the muffled sounds of what might have been a warning announcement.

But… But…

Mallory forced her mind to stop spinning in empty circles. She wasn't completely irresponsible. Nor was she helpless. She'd worked for the Commerce Department for several years before accepting the offer from Congressman Kent to join his staff. She understood bureaucracy, knew she had to get the wheels turning. Buttoning down her panic, she constructed a mental list.

First, she'd verify with the authorities here on Mont St. Michael that she was the driver of the vehicle that had been swept out to sea. She'd need statements from them and other witnesses as to what happened to the car when she contacted the rental agency. Then she'd call the U.S. embassy and find out how to obtain a temporary passport. After that, she'd get American Express to replace her lost traveler's checks. She'd also check with them about travel insurance and coverage for her lost suitcase and clothing.

Relieved to have a plan, Mallory turned to the man beside her. "Would you be willing to provide a written statement detailing how I, uh, lost the car?"

"Sure."

She swept a hand toward the stairs leading down to the village. "I need to let whoever's in charge around here know that was my vehicle. Then I need to make some calls. You don't happen to have a cell phone with you, do you?"

Something flickered in his cool gray eyes. Mallory thought it might have been amusement, but it was gone before she could be sure.

"As a matter of fact, I do."

"Would you mind if I use it?"

"Not at all."

"Thanks. Again," she added, embarrassed now by the memory of her less-than-cordial response when he'd tossed the tipsy tourist into the horse trough.

If he remembered it, he gave no sign. Matching his stride to hers, he accompanied her to the stairs leading to the exit from the hilltop abbey.

"My name is Cutter Smith, by the way."

Mallory hesitated. She could hardly refuse to provide her name after all he'd done for her, but anticipation of his reaction when he connected her to the headlines made her cringe inside.

"I'm Mallory Dawes."

"Nice to meet you, Mallory. I'm sorry it had to be under these circumstances."

His grip on her elbow was warm and sure and strong. His expression didn't telegraph so much as a flicker of recognition. Relieved, Mallory flashed him a smile.

"You and me both."

Chapter 4

Cutter had suspected she'd be a looker when she jettisoned her sour expression, but he'd underestimated the result by exponential degrees.

When Mallory Dawes smiled, she was more than mere eye candy. She was all warm, seductive woman. The smile softened her mouth and gave her cinnamon eyes a sparkling glow. It also damned near made Cutter miss his footing on the steep stairs.

Feeling as though he'd taken a hard fist to his chest, he recovered enough to escort her down a million or so zigzagging stairs and through the village to the main entrance. Mallory halted just outside the massive barbican gate, surveying the scene.

"I can't believe this. It's so…so surreal."

Cutter had to agree with her. The tide had swept in with a vengeance. Beyond the gate, the causeway shot straight and narrow across a broad expanse of silver-gray water. Except for that man-made strip of concrete, Mont St. Michel was completely cut off from the rest of France.

A large crowd lined the western edge of the causeway. Most were tourists busy clicking away with their cameras. Others looked like locals. Gesturing extravagantly, they shouted encouragement as a wrecker battled valiantly to keep Tour Bus 57 from being swept out to sea. They'd managed to attach tow chains to the bus and had it strung like a giant whale while it slowly took on water.

As Cutter and Mallory watched, transfixed, the sea reached the level of its windows and poured in through several that had been left open. The bus sank right before their eyes and settled in eight or ten feet of water, with only its top showing.

The tourists continued to shoot photo after photo. A man whose white shirt and nametag suggested he was the tour bus driver paced back and forth. Flinging his hands in the air and gesticulating wildly, he poured out a stream of impassioned French to a uniformed gendarme.

The officer took notes in a black notebook, somehow managing to look sympathetic and supremely bored at the same time. Cutter guessed he probably dealt with drivers of sunk or missing vehicles several times a week and had little sympathy for idiots who ignored warning signs and loudspeaker announcements.

Mallory had obviously formed that same impression. Chewing on her lower lip, she turned to Cutter. "This could get dicey. How's your French?"

"I can order a beer and ask directions to the bathroom. How's yours?"

"Two years in college. I can find my way around, but I never learned the proper phrase for 'My car is now at the bottom of the ocean.'"

"I think he'll get the drift."

"Hope so."

Actually, Cutter could communicate fairly fluently with authorities on several different continents. He'd already decided how to capitalize on this situation, however, and his plan didn't include making things easy for Ms. Dawes. Accordingly, he stayed in the background when she approached the police officer.

"*Excusez-moi.*"

"*Oui,* mademoiselle?"

"*Ma voiture, uh, été perdue.*"

At his blank look, she fell back on English and the universal language of hand gestures.

"My car. It's gone. Out there."

"*Oui,* mademoiselle." Heaving a long-suffering sigh, the officer hefted his notebook and pen. "Tell me, please, the license number."

"I don't know the license number."

"The make and year?"

"It was a Peugeot. A little one. Blue."

The gendarme was too well trained to roll his eyes, but it was obvious to everyone present he wanted to.

"You have rented this car, yes?"

"Yes. From an agency at the Paris airport."

"We shall call the rental agency and get the information I must have for my report. This way, *s'il vous plaît.*"

The glance Dawes threw Cutter's way sent a spear of intense satisfaction through him. He was an ally now. No longer a stranger, not quite a friend, but a familiar face in a sea of trouble. Ms. Dawes didn't know it, but they were about to get a whole lot better acquainted.

He nodded encouragement as she accompanied the gendarme to the police van parked at midpoint on the causeway. While the officer got on his radio and requested a connection to an operator at the Paris airport, Cutter eased out of sight at the rear of the van and made a call of his own.

Mike Callahan took his succinct report of the

sinking of the Peugeot along with the request he draw on Lightning's particular expertise.

On the other side of the Atlantic, Mike whipped around to check the electronic status board on the wall behind him. The blue light beside the director's name indicated Nick was alone and at his desk downstairs.

"Lightning's on scene," Mike advised Cutter. "I'll get back to you in ten."

"Roger that."

Shoving back from the console containing an array of screens and phones that would have made his counterparts in the CIA and FBI turn green with envy, Mike strode toward the elevator. The titanium-shielded bullet zoomed him down three stories with stomach-bouncing efficiency.

Grimacing at his reflection in the highly reflective door, Mike scrubbed a hand over his cheeks and chin. He'd been at the control desk without break since the op had kicked off. No big deal compared to some of the stretches he'd pulled. Still, he could have scraped off his whiskers during the down hours between contacts with Slash. There was a reason OMEGA maintained sleeping quarters, shower facilities and a fully-equipped gym for controllers and their backups.

Mike's mouth twisted. Hell! Who was he kidding? He'd never given a thought to his whiskers before. Nor had any other male operative, until a certain blue-eyed babe with a killer smile and a body to match had volunteered to fill in for the recuperating Elizabeth Wells.

He could see Gillian now, courtesy of the hidden cameras that made regular sweeps of the elegant first-floor offices. Although they appeared empty of visitors, Mike pressed a button to signal he wanted entry and waited for Lightning's temporary assistant to give him access.

Okay, he lectured himself sternly as the elevator door whooshed open. *All right.* No need to get his shorts in a bunch. He was thirty-five years old, for God's sake. He'd spent the past seven years as an OMEGA operative. When not dodging bullets, he trained sharpshooters for a list of agencies that read like a governmental alphabet soup.

No damned reason his insides should turn to mush because Adam Ridgeway's daughter swiveled around in her chair to greet him.

"Hi, Mike."

"Hi, Gillian-with-a-*J.*"

It was a stupid joke, one he'd pretty well worn out in the years since Adam had brought his coltish teenaged daughter to the shooting range and she'd solemnly introduced herself as Gillian, spelled-with-a-*G*-but-pronounced-with-a-*J.*

The teenager had gone on to graduate magna cum laude from Georgetown, had landed a job at the State

Department and snared a plum first assignment at the American Embassy in Beijing. Daddy's connections had no doubt had something to do with that. Mike suspected her Uncle Nick had probably weighed in, as well. Now Gillian was home between assignments, filling in for Elizabeth Wells for a few months and making Mike's life a living hell.

He was too old for her, he reminded himself for the hundredth time. Too damned rough around the edges. She'd grown up in the country-club set. He preferred not to think about the cesspool he'd sprung from. Rumor had it that she was getting snuggly with some buttoned-down Ivy League type, and that he was the reason she'd decided to take this hiatus before accepting another overseas assignment. That alone should have prevented Mike from going hard and tight when Gillian asked what she could do for him.

Should have, but didn't.

Ruthlessly suppressing several inappropriate thoughts of what he'd *like* her to do for him, he growled out a terse reply.

"I need to see Nick."

"Sure." Crossing one knee over the other, she reached for the intercom. "Hang on a sec."

Sweat popped out on Mike's palms. The girl—woman!—was all leg. Damned if she wasn't well aware of it, too.

Jilly hid a smile as she buzzed her godfather and honorary uncle. She knew she shouldn't tease Mike. Her father, mother *and* godfather would all lace into her if they had any idea she'd deliberately let her skirt slide up. Or that she was taunting an operative with Mike Callahan's reputation.

Problem was, she'd nursed a world-class crush on Callahan since he'd positioned her in front of him, wrapped his arms around her, and helped her line up a paper target in the sights of a Walther PPK. She just might have to take a refresher course, Jilly mused as Nick picked up.

"Hawkeye needs to see you," she advised.

"Send him in."

Exercising severe mental discipline, Mike put the long-legged temptress out of his head and gave his boss a quick update. Lightning's reaction was one of amusement.

"The car sank?"

"Like a rock. Slash says he saw it go under, taking Dawes's suitcase, passport and traveler's checks with it."

"I've been to Mont St. Michel a good number of times. Amazing what tourists leave in their cars while they trudge up to the abbey."

Every OMEGA agent knew the story. Nick Jensen, born Henri Nicolas Everaud, had once run numbers and picked pockets in his native France.

He'd also offered to pimp for Maggie Sinclair, Gillian's mother, during a long-ago op. Judging by the small smile that flitted across his face, he still had a hankering for the good ol' days.

"What about the disk?"

"It's still in the vehicle," Mike advised, "and sending signals."

"Does Slash think this business with the car was intentional? That the Russian will attempt an underwater retrieval?"

"If that's the plan, Slash doesn't believe Dawes was in on it. He says she's genuinely upset. Apparently," Mike added with a grin, "she's turned to him for help."

"I'm not going to ask how he managed that!"

"He wants to play the Good Samaritan and keep her on a string as long as possible. I've already made a call to State. Dawes won't get a replacement passport any time soon. I'll work American Express when I get back upstairs. What I need from you is a recommendation for a good spot for Slash to go to roost in the area."

"I know just the place."

His enigmatic smile returning, Nick lifted the phone.

"Jilly, please get me Madame Yvette d'Marchand."

"The shoe designer?"

"That's her." He checked his watch. "She's probably at her Paris office, on the Boulevard St.

Germain. If not, her secretary will know where she can be reached."

Mike walked out of Nick's office a few minutes later with directions to a seaside villa and assurances that its staff would be primed and ready to receive Monsieur Cutter Smith and companion.

Gillian-with-a-*J* gave him a wave and another glimpse of those mile-long legs. Mike's jaw had locked by the time the elevator door swished shut.

"A villa?"

Cutter threw a quick glance at the police van to make sure Mallory was still engaged with the gendarme.

"I was thinking more in terms of a hotel room where I could maintain close surveillance."

"So was I," Hawkeye relayed, "but Lightning says this place is airtight. The owner ran a string of high-class call girls until she married one of her clients and he set her up in another line of business. She's since made millions as a fashion designer. Lightning says she's an avid art collector, and has all of her homes equipped with start-of-the-art surveillance. You won't have to worry about security."

"What's my cover?"

"You're a wine broker, in France for the fall tastings and lot auctions. A friend of a friend knows the villa's owner. She offered to let you use it as a base while you search out select vintages in the

Calvados and Loire regions for your extremely discriminating clients."

"Hell, I don't know Calvados from Calvin Klein. You'd better zap me a short course in French wineries."

"It'll be waiting for you at the villa."

"Roger that. Gotta go. The target just parted company with our local gendarme and looks ready to bite nails."

Not just bite them, Cutter decided as he slipped the phone into his pocket. Chew them into little pieces.

"Problem?" he asked politely.

"Yes," she ground out. "The rental agency says they have to check with their insurance company before they can authorize another vehicle. They've also put a hold on my credit card until full damages and liability are assessed."

She raked back her hair, threading the silky strands through her fingers.

"Looks like I'm stuck here until American Express comes through. May I use your phone?"

Hawkeye had promised to take care of American Express; Cutter needed to give him time to work it.

"Sure, but you'll need something to write with once you get hold of the information. I've got a pen in my car. It's right over there."

He lowered the windows to let the sea breeze in while she struggled with the information operator.

She couldn't know every word was being recorded, or that Cutter derived a sardonic enjoyment from her mounting frustration.

"I know I should have made a record of the check numbers," she said after a short exchange with whomever she'd reached, "but I didn't. Can't you look me up in the computer?"

She waited, tapping her borrowed pen against the notepad Cutter had thoughtfully provided.

"You did! Thank God!"

The happy grin she zinged Cutter's way lit up her face. Seconds later, the grin collapsed.

"No, I can't come to the Paris office to present my passport as identification. I'm currently without cash and any means of transportation. I'm also without passport."

Another lengthy pause.

"Excuse me, but we're not communicating here. It doesn't matter where the closest American Express office is. I don't have the money to get to Paris *or* Nantes *or* Marseilles and I've lost my passport along with my traveler's checks."

Her expression grew more thunderous by the second.

"Yes, I understand you're not authorized to fork over the funds without proper identification. Can't I go to a bank or post office? Or a notary. You have notaries in France, don't you? He or she could verify my ID from my driver's license and fax you the verification. No. No, I don't. Oh, for heaven's sake! Hold on."

Her eyes stormy, she appealed to Cutter.

"He has to get authorization from his superiors to accept a notarized signature. It may take a little time. He needs a number where he can contact me."

"Give him mine."

Magnanimously, Cutter jotted it down for her. She relayed it to the clerk and snapped the cell phone shut. Her glance strayed to the island looming just yards away.

"Lord, I hope there's a notary somewhere on that pile of rock."

He let her down gently. "You might have to look farther afield. I read somewhere that Mont St. Michel has only about fifty or so permanent residents."

He made that up to twist the screws a little tighter. It worked. Dawes's muttered expletive would have done any of the OMEGA operatives proud. Glancing sideways, she caught Cutter's grin and colored.

"Sorry. I'm, uh, a little rattled by all this."

"Not to worry," he chuckled. "I've heard worse."

Mallory would bet he had. His expertly tailored sports coat and Italian loafers shouted money, but she'd seen the man in action. He'd handled the beefy tourist who'd accosted her with unruffled ease. She suspected he hadn't come by those powerful shoulders working out in a gym. Then there were those awful scars....

Wondering how he'd acquired them, she flipped up his cell phone again. The sun was a red ball slipping toward the sea. She'd better finish her calls and find some place to stay the night.

All too well aware that a hotel or inn would require a guest's passport, she wrestled the number for the American Embassy from the information operator. The embassy was closed, but a recording gave her a twenty-four-hour emergency number. Unfortunately, the duty officer who answered didn't classify a lost passport in the same emergency category as death, dismemberment or attack by suicide bombers.

Mallory argued the point for some minutes before gritting her teeth and informing him she would call back tomorrow. *During* duty hours.

"God! Bureaucrats! I can't believe I'm one of them. Or was," she amended darkly.

Snapping the phone shut, she handed it back to Cutter. What the heck was she going to do now?

Spend the night sitting at a table in one of the little bistros, she supposed, if she could find one that stayed open twenty-four hours. Judging by the departing tour buses and rapidly emptying causeway, Mont St. Michel was a day-tripper's town. Mallory had the sinking feeling it rolled up its streets at night.

Cutter's deep voice dragged her from the dismal prospect of roaming dark alleys and narrow lanes in search of a spot to rest her weary bones.

"I don't like leaving you stranded like this."

"I'll manage."

Somehow.

"How about we walk back into the town and get you a hotel room for the night?"

Mallory was too relieved to mouth even a polite refusal. "Would you? I'll reimburse you, I promise. Just give me your business card or mailing address."

"No problem. Or…"

When he hesitated, her heart sank. Visions of dark alleys once again filled her head.

"Look, you're going to need a base camp for a few days to get this mess straightened out. I've been invited to put up at a villa not far from here. You're welcome to stay there for as long as you like."

Wariness replaced weariness. Her face stiffening, Mallory retreated behind the defensive walls she'd erected in the past month. "Thanks, but I don't think so."

As if reading her mind, he gentled his voice.

"It's okay. I'm not like the jerk who harassed you this afternoon. I promise I won't hit on you."

A smile crinkled the skin at the corners of his eyes.

"Unless you want me to."

Chapter 5

Doubts pinged at Mallory during the thirty-minute drive to the villa.

Cutter's invitation had seemed genuine enough. So had his promise to keep his hands to himself. She wanted to believe him. She was too exhausted *not* to. Yet the ugliness of the past month kept coming back to haunt her.

What if he'd recognized her from the vicious stories in the newspapers and on TV? Or overheard the nasty remarks that creep had tossed out this afternoon? Mallory's ready capitulation and acceptance of his offer to share a villa would have reinforced the rumors of her alleged promiscuity.

On the other hand...

He'd come to her rescue twice now, each time with quiet and extremely effective competence. Despite her prickly doubts and still-raw wounds, she felt comfortable with him. And, as crazy as it sounded, safe.

Besides, she didn't have a basketful of options at this point. Every bone in her body ached with weariness. All she wanted was a bed. Any kind of a bed.

"You said you're a bureaucrat. Or were."

His voice came to her through the autumn dusk now filling the car's interior.

"What kind of work did you do?"

She dragged herself from her near-catatonic state and searched for an answer that wouldn't open Pandora's box.

"I worked at the U.S. Department of Commerce for five years."

And then she'd accepted the position on Congressman Kent's staff.

Lord, what a mistake that had been! But Dillon Porter, Kent's senior staffer, had lured her up to the Hill with tantalizing visions of helping shape laws and policies that would affect the nation's balance of trade for decades to come.

"Commerce, huh? What did you do there?"

"Nothing very glamorous. I was an analyst with the Market Access and Compliance Branch of the International Trade Administration. Basically, I crunched numbers to track U.S. exports to and imports from Canada."

"Sounds like a big job."

"It certainly kept me busy. More than half a trillion dollars in goods flow between the U.S. and Canada every year. Most of the trade is dispute-free, although things got dicey for a while over softwood lumber." A note of pride crept into her voice. "I helped draft the agreement that finally settled that decades-long dispute."

"I'm impressed."

Looking back, Mallory had to admit that was her finest hour. She'd played a minuscule role in the landmark agreement, mostly providing historical trending stats, but her input had been valuable enough to win her a spot at the signing ceremony. It had also brought her to the attention of the House Committee on Banking and Trade.

How swiftly the proud can fall. Swallowing a sigh, Mallory skirted that dangerous ground.

"You said you're a wine broker. How often do you log onto the International Trade Administration's database?"

"When I need to."

The vague reply aroused her professional pride.

"You should check the database regularly. ITA updates it daily with the latest data on markets and products. You can also use that system to report unfair competition and dumping by foreign competitors."

Cutter was on shaky ground here. What he knew about the Department of Commerce and the International Trade Administration would make for an extremely short conversation. If he didn't want to trip himself up, he'd better steer the conversation into different channels...like Ms. Dawes's most recent occupation.

"I'm surprised you stayed at Commerce for so long. From what I've seen as an outsider looking in, a good number of Washington's brightest bureaucrats get lured into the political arena and end up either as lobbyists or working on a Congressional staff."

Her glance was quick and suspicious. Cutter kept his eyes on the road ahead and let her mull over her answer. A signpost at the juncture of the road gave her an out.

"Look, there's the turnoff for St. Malo. Don't your directions say the villa is only two kilometers ahead, on the right?"

"On the left," he corrected.

He'd let her off the hook for now. With Hawk back at OMEGA control, inserting spikes into every wheel, she wasn't going anywhere soon. Cutter would have plenty of time to worm Ms. Dawes's secrets out of her.

"Looks like this may be the place," he announced after a few minutes.

Slowing his rental, he pulled up at a set of iron gates decorated with gilded scrollwork and mythological creatures. Cutter noted with approval the tamper-proof screens protecting the security cameras mounted above the gate. Pressing the call button, he identified himself to the disembodied voice that answered.

"*Bon soir,* Monsieur Smith. We have been expecting you."

The gates swung open to reveal a long drive that wound through acres of manicured lawn and led to a château perched on the rocky cliffs overlooking the sea. Complete with towers and turrets, the castle was right out of the fifteenth century.

Mallory's jaw dropped. Cutter caught his just in time.

"This is your seaside villa?" she asked incredulously.

"I, ah, heard about it through a friend of a friend. He didn't indicate it was this grandiose."

Crushed stone crunched under the tires. Cutter's trained eye detected more cameras mounted at strategic intervals and the glint of what he suspected were passive sensors laced throughout the grounds.

The drive ended at an arched passageway that once might have contained a portcullis. The passageway gave access to an inner courtyard. Two individuals waited inside the walled yard. The one on the right was tall and lean, with short-cropped salt-and-pepper hair, a neat mustache and a dignified air. Coming forward with a stately tread, he assisted Mallory from the car and introduced himself as Gilbért Picard, the majordomo and property overseer. With him was his wife, Madame Picard, a shy, rotund woman with rosy cheeks.

Gilbért was as smooth as butter and didn't so much as bat an eyelash when Cutter emerged from the vehicle. His wife's startled gaze went instantly to the scars, however. Just as quickly, she looked away.

Used to the reaction, Cutter introduced himself and Mallory. Gilbért apologized for paucity of staff here to greet them and retrieved Cutter's carryall from the trunk. If he wondered at Mallory's lack of baggage, he was too well trained to comment on it.

"Madame brings her maid and masseuse when she travels down from Paris," he explained, leading the way inside. "We have two girls from the village who come each day to clean. I will ask one to see to Mademoiselle Dawes's personal needs, *oui?*"

"I don't need a maid," Mallory protested. "Just a place to crash."

"Pardon?"

"All I want is a bed."

"But of course."

With a measured tread, he led them down a long

hall wainscoted in glowing golden oak. The alcoves lining the hall contained ultramodern sculptures with sharp angles and odd shapes. The pieces should have looked out of place in this ancient castle, but old and new somehow blended seamlessly.

Mallory peeked through open doors as they passed, stealing glimpses of salons and sitting rooms and a library stacked floor to ceiling with books bound in leather and etched with gold print on the spines. The grand ballroom and music room were on the second floor, the guest rooms and madame's private suite on the third.

On this floor, as on the others, both past and present came vividly alive. Baronial banners with richly embroidered coats of arms hung above suits of armor gilded with silver and gold. Yet the place of honor went to a Picasso spotlighted above a refectory table that might once have graced a twelfth-century cloister.

"We have put mademoiselle in the blue bedchamber," Picard announced as he opened an ornate set of double doors halfway down the corridor. "I hope it will be satisfactory."

Mallory stepped inside and felt as though she'd wandered into a Mediterranean grotto. *Blue* hardly described the shimmering azure of the drapes and upholstered chairs in the sitting room, or the richly embroidered coverlet on the four-poster bed. The bathroom beyond was accented with lapis lazuli trim, gold fixtures and sinks shaped like seashells. As in the rest of the château, modern sculpture and artwork coexisted beautifully with antique furniture.

"Monsieur is in the green chamber, next door."

Picard made no reference to the connecting doors between the two suites.

"Do you wish the dinner before you retire?" he asked politely. "Something light, perhaps? The omelette? Or the vol-au-vent, with fresh asparagus and our most delicious Normandy mussels?"

"Well…"

Hunger and exhaustion waged a fierce war using Mallory as the battleground. Her stomach beat the rest of her into submission. The lunch in Caen had been delicious, but hardly filling.

"The vol-au-vent sounds wonderful. If it's not too much trouble…"

"Not at all. Madame Picard baked the pastry shells only this afternoon. I shall tell her to set a table in the petite dining salon. In thirty minutes, *oui?*"

Mallory would have preferred a tray here in her room, but awareness of how much she owed Cutter made her reluctant to appear rude. Or too demanding of his time, she thought belatedly.

"Please don't let me alter any arrangements you've made for this evening," she said with a smile. "I'll be fine here. *More* than fine," she amended, making another sweep of the elegant bedchamber.

"All I had planned for this evening was to catch up on some paperwork. I'll see you downstairs in thirty minutes."

He disappeared with Gilbért, leaving Mallory to shrug out of her blazer and head for the bathroom. To her delight, an enameled casket offered a selection of shampoos, scented soaps, body lotions, bath gels and tooth powders. The thoughtful hostess had even provided her guests toothbrushes in hygienically sealed containers. A twenty-first-century hair dryer and lighted mirror shared space on the dressing table with a silver-backed brush, comb and hand mirror that might once have belonged to Marie Antoinette.

Mallory ached to sink into the tub but settled for a quick shower. Wrapping herself in one of the fluffy robes hanging in the closet, she slathered on lotion delicately scented with lilies of the valley. The creamy lotion moistened her skin and permeated the bath with flowery perfume.

Once back in the bedroom, she cringed at the prospect of pulling on the same clothes she'd worn for more than twenty hours. Madame Picard's arrival obviated that necessity.

"*Pardonnez-moi,* mademoiselle. Monsieur Smith says you have lost your suitcase to the tides at Mont St. Michel. They are so treacherous, these tides." Tsk-tsking, she shook her head and held out an arm draped with garments. "Madame keeps a spare wardrobe here at the château. These items, I think, will fit you."

"Oh, no! I couldn't."

"But you must. Madame d'Marchand would be most displeased if Gilbért and I did not see to the comfort of her guests."

Overcoming Mallory's protests, she laid the garments on the bed. The gown and matching negligee were lavender silk, lavishly trimmed with blond lace. The briefs and demi-bra were also silk.

For outerwear, Madame Picard provided a gorgeously patterned blouse by Hermès and nutmeg-colored slacks in fine Italian merino wool. She'd even thought to bring a pair of net anklets still in their plastic wrapper.

"Madame sells these in her boutiques," she advised Mallory. "You will wish to wear them with these, yes?"

From her pocket she produced a pair of slip-on mules in a leopard print splashed with bright red geraniums. The shiny metallic heels were the same eye-popping red and shaped like hourglasses. When Mallory glimpsed the label inside the mules, the light came on with blinding brilliance.

"Omigod! Is your Madame d'Marchand the shoe designer, Yvette d'Marchand?"

"*Oui.*" Pride beamed across the housekeeper's face. "You have visited her boutique in Paris? Or in New York, on Fifth Avenue?"

"No, I haven't."

Like Mallory could afford a pair of shoes by Yvette d'Marchand! Movie stars and presidents' wives engaged in fierce bidding wars over her one-of-a-kind designs.

"Perhaps you can arrange a visit before you leave Paris," the housekeeper suggested, depositing the shoes beside the garments. "The petite dining salon is in the conservatory. Monsieur Smith awaits you there. It is just beyond the main dining salon."

"Thanks."

Mallory debated for all of thirty seconds before sloughing off the robe and sliding into the decadent briefs. The matching bra was too large, so she left it off and just went with a silky camisole. The shoes needed a little tissue at the toes, but otherwise fit beautifully.

Amazing how a shower and a pair of designer shoes could revive a girl!

Weary but rejuvenated, Mallory descended the stairs and followed Madame Picard's directions through the main dining salon. Four magnificent Limoges chandeliers graced the banquet-hall-sized room, which featured a still life that had to be the work of Paul Gauguin. French doors lined one side of the room and gave onto the glassed-in conservatory.

Mallory paused just inside the French doors, taking in the splendor of the setting. The conservatory's fanciful Victorian ironwork, profusion of potted plants and fan-backed wicker chairs produced a gloriously decadent belle epoque feel, while the glass walls provided an unobstructed view of the Normandy coast, now fading into the dusk.

A breathtakingly beautiful chess table set with ivory and ebony pieces occupied place of honor amid scattered lounge chairs at one end of the conservatory. The petite dining salon occupied the other. The round, glass-topped wicker table was set with linen and an array of covered dishes. Candles flickered in tall silver holders. Crystal water goblets sparkled in the candles' glow.

Cutter stood at the windows close to the table. A highball glass in hand, he appeared riveted by the spectacle of incandescent waves crashing against the rocky coast. He'd showered, too, Mallory saw. His short dark hair curled in still-damp waves and the bristles that had darkened his cheeks were gone. He'd traded his sport coat and shirt for a silky black turtleneck that molded his wide shoulders and, coincidentally or otherwise, hid most of his scars.

What in the world was she doing here? Mallory wondered, in this fairy-tale castle, about to have dinner with this stranger? The ordeal of the past weeks had made her gun-shy and wary around men. With good reason. She couldn't count the number of sly innuendos and outright insults she'd endured since becoming the butt of so many raunchy jokes tossed out by late-night talk-show hosts.

Even if the media hadn't made her a target, she would have had second thoughts if she'd encountered Cutter Smith on an empty street or in a deserted parking lot. Despite his expensive loafers and superbly cut sport coat, he carried himself with a tough, don't-mess-with-me air that would have made Mallory give him a wide berth.

Yet, after knowing the man for all of four or five hours, she'd driven off with him to this isolated château and was about to sit down to an intimate, candlelight dinner for two. Worse, she found herself wanting to trust him, wanting to believe he really was as kind and considerate as he seemed to be.

Not that it mattered. They'd go their separate ways tomorrow. For tonight, though, maybe she could let down her guard enough to simply enjoy his company.

The sound of her borrowed mules clicking against the tiles brought his head around. When he took in her altered appearance, a smile softened the harsh lines of his face.

"I see Madame Picard came through for you."

"Yes, she did. Thanks for mentioning my lost suitcase, although I have to confess I feel odd invading our hostess's home *and* wardrobe. Did your friend of a friend tell you what she does for a living?"

"He mentioned she designs clothing."

"Not clothing." Tugging up one leg of her borrowed Italian wool slacks, she waggled her foot. "Shoes. Hand-crafted, one-of-a-kind, thousand-dollars-a-pair shoes."

"Mmm," Cutter murmured, eyeing the slender ankle above the flashy leopard-and-red slipper. "Nice."

When she finished waggling and he'd finished admiring, he nodded toward the array of crystal decanters on a sideboard framed by feathery palms.

"Would you like a drink before dinner? Or wine? Gilbért brought a very nice Pouilly-Fuissé up from the cellars."

He had his spiel all prepared. As requested, Hawkeye had assembled and text-messaged several cheat sheets he'd labeled Wine for Dummies. If Mallory asked, Cutter was all set to expound on the dry, medium-bodied white wine from the Burgundy region of France. Made from the chardonnay grape, Pouilly-Fuissé was not to be confused with Pouilly-Fumé, made from the sauvignon blanc grape variety in the southeastern portion of the Loire Valley.

Thankfully, she didn't ask.

"I'd better pass on both. As tired as I am, alcohol might land me face down in the vol-au-vent. Which," she added, sniffing at the tantalizing aroma emanating from the covered dishes on the table, "smells incredible."

Cutter could take a hint when it whapped him in the face. Grinning, he set his drink aside. "Shall we eat, then? I told Gilbért we'd serve ourselves."

"Yes, please!"

When he went around to pull out her chair, he had to admit she smelled every bit as good as their dinner. Her skin carried a faint, flowery scent that reminded him of alpine meadows in spring.

"Want me to do the honors?" she asked when he'd taken the seat opposite.

"Be my guest."

While she wielded silver tongs and ladles, Cutter stretched his legs out under the table and revised his strategy. He'd planned to loosen her up with wine, charm her over a drawn-out dinner, and get her talking. The utter fatigue underlying her movements told him he'd better speed things up or she might fall asleep here at the table.

She helped by taking the lead. First she filled two plates with pastry shells topped by cream sauce swimming with chunks of mussels and fish, then added spears of tender white asparagus. Passing one plate to Cutter, she picked at the other.

"I'm curious," she commented. "How did you get into the wine business?"

"By accident."

That was true enough.

"I pulled a couple of hitches in the Army. During

one of them, I was stationed at a small site in Germany. I got to know the locals pretty well."

That was true, as well. His gut tightening at the thought of one particular local, Cutter ruthlessly slammed the door on the memory of the traitorous bitch who'd almost incinerated him before he'd taken her down.

Would this one try something equally desperate?

"One of the people I got to know was a wine wholesaler," he told Mallory, improvising from that point on. "We kept in touch after I left Germany. When I was looking for something to do after I left the Army, I contacted him and we went into partnership."

She speared a tender mussel with her fork but didn't bring it to her lips. "What did you do in the Army?"

He knew what she was edging around and decided to bring it out in the open.

"I trained as an explosive ordnance specialist before I transferred to the Rangers. Thought I knew all there was to know about cluster bombs, combined effects munitions and IEDs. Individual Explosive Devices," he translated at her blank look. "Turns out I didn't know as much as I thought. One of 'em blew away half my face."

He didn't add that the IED was part of a cache of stolen weapons he'd been tracking...or that his NATO partner on that op was a cool Scandinavian beauty who'd been playing a dangerous double game that had ended when their collaboration literally blew up in Cutter's face.

Months of reconstructive surgery and skin grafts had followed. The docs had wanted to do more, but Cutter had finally called a halt. He'd left the Army soon afterward, lured to OMEGA by Mike Callahan. His first mission had been to track down the woman who'd betrayed him and her country. Now, all these years later, he was working the same kind of op with another blonde.

Almost the same, he amended. His gut told him Mallory Dawes was at best an unwitting accomplice, at worst a mule transporting something she didn't know the value of. He'd watched her every move, listened to every nuance in her voice when her car sank. She'd panicked, sure, but the only real concern she'd expressed was for her passport and traveler's checks. There'd been none over her suitcase or what it contained.

Until Cutter knew how the disk had found its way into her suitcase, however, he wasn't ready to let her off the hook…or out of his sight. Smoothly, he redirected the thread of their conversation.

"I have to admit, I'm enjoying my new line of work more than the old. I've got an appointment with a local vintner tomorrow morning. Why don't you come with me?"

"I'd love to, but I can't. I need to find a notary and

fax my signature to the American Express office. And follow up with the embassy about my passport. And sort out this mess with the rental-car agency."

"I'm sure Gilbért knows the location of a notary. We'll stop by and obtain his or her chop on the way to the vintner. You can make any calls you need to on my cell phone."

"Thanks, but I've already imposed on you too much."

"Why don't you sleep on it? We'll talk again in the morning."

"Speaking of sleep..."

Her shoulders sagging, she laid down her fork. She'd taken only a few bites of her dinner. Cutter could see that was all she'd manage. The color had seeped from her cheeks and left them gray with fatigue.

"I'm afraid I'll have to poop out on you. Jet lag is catching up with a vengeance."

"No problem." He rose and came around to slide back her chair. "I'll see you tomorrow. Sleep well, Mallory."

"You, too."

As she turned to face him, her flowery scent teased his senses again. Cutter resisted the urge to brush a wayward strand of corn-silk hair off her cheek. If her allegations against Congressman Kent held even a grain of truth, Ms. Dawes didn't take kindly to being touched.

He wanted to, though, with a sudden, gut-twisting

urgency that surprised the hell out of him. Controlling the urge, he stepped away from her.

Cutter Smith wasn't like the others.

The thought teased at Mallory's tired mind as she dragged up the stairs.

She'd seen that spark of heat in his eyes a few moments ago. Felt the sudden, subtle tension sizzle through the air between them. But he'd promised she'd be safe with him.

He'd also promised he wouldn't hit on her unless she wanted him to. Now here she was, wishing she'd given him the green light.

Was she an idiot, or what?

Chapter 6

Still on Central American jungle time, Cutter's internal alarm failed to go off in time for his usual dawn run. He didn't jerk awake until his cell phone buzzed.

The ring tone sounded ordinary enough, but he was so attuned to the sequence of musical notes that he went from total unconsciousness to fully alert in two seconds flat.

"Yeah, I know," Mike Callahan said when his craggy face appeared on the screen. "It's early as hell."

"It is for me," Cutter agreed, scraping a hand over his chin. "Late as hell for you."

Callahan must have stayed at Control a second

night in a row. Wondering what had kept him there, Cutter threw off the duvet and swung upright. He'd left the windows open to the sea breeze last night. The air carried a damp bite this morning, but that wasn't what prickled the skin of his bare chest and arms. Callahan wouldn't have initiated contact without good reason.

"What's up, Hawk?"

"Thought you might want to know about your friend, Walters."

Cutter's mind clicked instantly to the heavyset tourist who'd accosted Mallory yesterday. Robert Walters. Age: fifty-three. Siding and storm doors. High roller.

"Did you pull his phone records?"

"I did," Mike confirmed. "Found some very interesting threads, but that's not why I contacted you. I intercepted State Department message traffic a few hours ago. The Bureau of Consular Affairs is trying to locate Walters's next-of-kin. Seems he met with an unfortunate accident yesterday, a few hours after your run-in with him."

"What kind of an accident?"

"He tumbled down some steps at Mont St. Michel and broke his neck."

An image of the steep, narrow passageways cut into solid rock flashed into Cutter's head. The steps were accidents waiting to happen, particularly to unwary tourists who'd imbibed one glass too many in a local bistro.

"What do the preliminary police reports say?"

"Although they're treating it as a 'suspicious' death and conducting a full investigation, they've found no witnesses or evidence to indicate the fall was anything but accidental. The inventory of the deceased's personal effects raised a red flag at *Direction Centrale,* however."

The hair on the back of Cutter's neck lifted. France's central director of police also served as head of their Interpol Bureau. As such, he played an integral role in combating international organized crime.

"Turns out our boy Walters had a soggy piece of paper in his wallet. The writing on it was blurred and almost obliterated…"

Surprise, surprise, Cutter thought wryly.

"…but they managed to lift an address. It checks to a small-time hood in Marseilles with suspected ties to the Russian."

"Well, hell!"

"I thought that might be your reaction," Mike drawled. "I checked the schedule of the tour Walters and his buddies were on. After visiting the Normandy beaches, they were scheduled to cut south to Bordeaux, then west to Marseilles before hitting the Riviera and the casino at Monaco."

Gripping the phone, Cutter paced to the windows.

The heavy drapes were open, the gauzy curtains fluttering in the damp breeze. He barely registered the chill blowing in as his mind ran with the possibilities.

Had Walters's horny tourist bit been an act? Was he the go-between designated to retrieve the disk from Mallory, either with or without her knowledge? Had he been instructed to deliver it to this thug in Marseilles?

If so, Cutter had interfered by busting up that little scene in the alley. After which, he'd spirited Mallory away and sequestered her here in this isolated château.

Then Walters had tumbled down a flight of steep steps. Was it an accident, or retribution for failing to retrieve the disk?

The last possibility presupposed the Russian had someone else shadowing Walters and/or Mallory. If so, had that someone witnessed her car floating out to sea? Did they know the disk was still in the trunk?

Dammit! It irritated the hell out of Cutter that he still had a *helluva* lot more questions than answers. Not the least of which was Mallory Dawes's role in all of this.

"You haven't had any movement on the disk, have you?" he asked Mike.

"Negative. It's still resting at the bottom of the sea. I've confirmed that the rental agency isn't going to attempt to raise the Peugeot, by the way. A salvage operation would cost more than the car is worth."

Frowning, Cutter turned away from the window and marshaled his thoughts.

"Okay, here's how I want to handle this. First, I'll work from the assumption that Walters was the designated go-between, sent to retrieve the disk from Dawes and deliver it to this thug in Marseilles. Second, I'm going to assume his death was no accident. That means there was someone else on scene, someone who engineered Walters's fall, either in retribution or anger over his bungled attempt. Third, unless and until a diver tries to retrieve the disk from the submerged vehicle, I'm assuming whoever wants the damned thing believes Dawes had it with her when she trudged up the ramp at Mont St. Michel to rendezvous with Walters."

"In which case, that someone has to believe she's still got it with her."

"Exactly."

"So you're going to use her as bait."

It wasn't a question, nor was there a hint of censure in Mike's voice. Cutter knew Hawk would do exactly the same given the circumstances. Staking out suspects like sacrificial goats was all part of the job. Cutter just wished this particular goat wasn't starting to get to him. He hadn't forgotten the fierce urge to touch her that had gripped him last night.

"Don't see that I have much choice," he bit out. "This place is a modern-day fortress. The Russian can't get to Mallory or the disk here. I'm taking her with me on my 'business' call to the local vintner you set me up with this morning."

"You got the cheat sheets I sent you, right?"

"Right. Good thing you warned me the Calvados region is more known for its brandy than its wine."

"That came from Lightning. Evidently this Monsieur Villieu provides private stock for Nick's restaurants. He said for you to confirm his order for the entire lot of 1989 Prestige blend, by the way."

Cutter was more of a beer-and-pretzels man than a brandy aficionado. If Nick Jensen wanted the entire stock of this stuff for his string of high-priced restaurants, though, it had to be something special.

When Cutter followed the aroma of fresh-brewed coffee to the petite dining salon some time later, he found Mallory ensconced in one of the fan-backed wicker chairs. The mist was fast burning off the cliffs outside but Cutter didn't spare the spectacular view a glance. His attention was centered on the woman slathering butter on a flaky croissant.

"Good morning."

When she looked up, her smile was warm and welcoming and plowed right into him. "Good morning."

"How do you feel?"

"Like a new woman."

He had to admit she looked like one, too. She

wore the same outfit she'd had on last night: jewel-toned blouse, slim brown slacks, frou-frouey shoes. But she'd swept her hair up into a twist that showed the smooth, clean line of her neck and jaw.

Her cheeks had regained their color, he noted. The gray tinge of exhaustion was gone. So was the wariness that had kept her voice cool and reserved. If she had lost sleep over a bungled exchange with Robert Walters, Cutter couldn't see any sign of it.

Filling a demitasse cup with coffee strong enough to substitute for roof tar, he carried the cup to the glass-topped wicker table. Mallory eyed the undiluted coffee with a raised brow.

"Don't you want some cream in that? It's high-octane."

"No, thanks."

Cutter welcomed the jolt to his central nervous system. After Mike's call, he needed it. While he ingested the caffeine, his breakfast companion nudged a basket of croissants and a small brown crock across the table.

"Well, you *have* to try this apple butter. Madame Picard says it's made from apples grown here in Normandy. After my first taste, I regretted every nasty word I muttered when I was stuck behind all those tractors hauling the fall harvest yesterday."

Cutter took advantage of the opening she'd just handed him to segue into his role. "That's not all they make from apples around here. The vintner I'm going to visit this morning produces some of the world's finest grape-based apple brandy."

"Grape-based apple brandy? Sounds almost like a contradiction in terms."

"It does, doesn't it?" Tearing apart a still-warm roll, he loaded it with creamy butter. "The appointment is for ten-thirty, but I can slip that if we need more time to locate a notary."

"Oh," she mumbled around a mouthful. "About that."

She flicked her tongue over her lower lip to capture a stray crumb. Cutter followed the movement with an intensity that annoyed the hell out of him.

"I really don't want to impose on you or your time. I'll get Gilbért to drive me to town."

Not hardly, he thought. He wasn't letting Ms. Dawes out of his sight.

"No sense both of us driving that way."

He took a bite and felt his taste buds leap for joy. Swallowing, he stared at the other half of his croissant.

"My God! This stuff is amazing."

Mallory had to grin at the expression on his face. He looked like a kid who'd just discovered a hidden stash of chocolate.

"Told you," she said smugly.

When he took another bite, the play of his throat muscles drew her gaze. He was wearing the silky black turtleneck again, paired with tan pleated slacks and a leather belt holding his clipped-on cell phone. The turtleneck covered most of the scars, but enough remained visible to tug at Mallory's heart.

She could only imagine the agony he must have suffered when the bomb he'd told her about last night exploded, taking part of his face with it. Thinking about his anguish, about how he must have had to fight for his life, made Mallory's own ordeal seem trivial by comparison. Slowly, inexorably, the tight knot of fury she'd carried around inside her for so many weeks loosened. As the knot unraveled, chagrin replaced the bitter, corrosive anger.

How stupid she'd been to lose all perspective the way she had! How egotistical to think her problems were so earth-shattering. People all over the world were battling cancer or dying of starvation or losing all they owned to war or the ravages of nature.

Yet here she sat, bathed in bright Norman sunlight, munching on warm croissants and apple butter, in the company of the most intriguing male she'd met in longer than she could remember. She'd be fifty times a fool not to savor every moment of this escape from harsh reality.

Those thoughts were still tumbling through her mind when Cutter downed the rest of his croissant and swiped his napkin across his mouth.

"That settles it. If the locals can work this kind of

magic with apples and butter, imagine what they can do with apples and brandy. You're going with me this morning."

Mallory capitulated with a rippling laugh. She'd tackle the American Embassy and the rental-car agency this afternoon. For now, she'd savor the bright sunshine and Cutter Smith's company.

"Okay, I'm going with you this morning. Let's get directions from Gilbért on how to find a notary."

Mallory hadn't counted on the French propensity for ignoring posted schedules.

Despite Gilbért's call to confirm the office hours of the town clerk, Mallory and Cutter sat on a bench and waited for more than twenty minutes for *le notaire* to pedal up. He offered a nonchalant apology, stuffed his beret into his jacket pocket, and led them to an office musty with the smell of old documents and wood imbued with damp from the salt-laden sea breeze.

To Mallory's relief, a computer and fax sat side-by-side with ranks of cloth-bound ledgers that looked as though they were left over from the 1800s. The clerk booted up and set out the tools of his trade.

"You wish me to witness your signature, yes?"

"Yes. Then I need to fax the authentication to the American Express office in Paris."

"*Bien.*" He waved her to the chair beside his desk. "We begin."

While he and Mallory took care of business, Cutter wandered over to examine an array of yellowed photos displayed on one wall. Mallory joined him a few moments later. One glimpse at the photographs explained his grim absorption.

The stark, unretouched images portrayed the epic battles that had raged along the beaches to the north during the Second World War. Coils of wire gleamed in the gray light, encircling turrets. Anti-aircraft artillery peeked from cement blockhouses. Machine-gun emplacements sat perched high on rocky ledges. And far below, at the base of the cliffs, row after row of lethal steel spears protruded from the surf.

"My grandfather takes these photos," the clerk said, coming to stand beside them. "He was an old man, you understand, and crippled, but he bicycles north to Côte de Nacre—what you call Omaha Beach—to make photos of German defenses and provide them to *la résistance*."

His chest puffing with pride, the clerk directed their attention to a framed document.

"General Eisenhower sends my grandfather a letter after the war and thanks him for his pictures. He says they helped to liberate our country. I have the copy here, but the original is in the museum at Arromanches."

Cutter dragged his gaze from the document and swept it over the photos again. As a former Ranger, he knew the history. The initial wave of the First Infantry Division, the Big Red One, had hit Omaha Beach at 0630. The second wave came ashore at 0700. The Rangers and the 116th Infantry regiment landed two hours later and were forced to wade through the bodies of their comrades before they finally cracked a breach in the German defenses. Supported by tanks and two destroyers delivering continuous bombardment, the Americans pushed through the breach and liberated the surrounding towns by the late afternoon.

"You will visit the museum?" the clerk asked. "And the American Cemetery? It is not far, on the road between St. Laurent and Colleville-sur-Mer."

With real regret, Cutter shook his head. "We'll have to visit the museum another day. This morning we go to Villieu Vintners."

"Ahhhh!" His face folding into paroxysms of delight, the clerk kissed his fingers. "You will sample the finest of Calvados brandies at Villieu. The best in all of France."

Afterward, Mallory was never quite sure how the day slipped away from her. She'd fully intended to return to the château by noon, untangle her affairs, and resume her interrupted vacation.

But after a short stop in the village so she could purchase a few items of clothing and toiletries, they drove northeast toward St. Lo. The dappled sunlight sifting through the trees wiped away much of Mallory's guilt that she wasn't back at the château, working the phones. Monsieur Villieu's ebullience and generous hospitality washed away the rest.

Or it could have been his brandy. The tingling scent of potent spirits surrounded her the moment she and Cutter arrived at the stone buildings housing Villieu et Fils Distillery.

Lean and spare, with cheeks chafed red by wind and sun, Villieu beamed as he walked his visitors through vineyards first planted by the Romans and orchards groaning with the weight of their fruit.

"The grapes, they do not grow as fat here as they do in Bordeaux and Cognac. The climate is too damp, the soil too flinty. Aaah, but when we blend our tough little grape with the apple and the pear…"

He kissed his fingers and opened the door to the fermenting sheds with a flourish. A sour-mash smell rose in waves from the huge vats and almost knocked Mallory back a step. Nose wrinkling, eyes watering, she breathed through her mouth until they exited the fermenting shed and entered a different world.

Here it was the heat that hit like a slap to the face. Sweat beading on her temples, Mallory followed Monsieur Villieu along rows of copper pots that looked like big, squat gourds with long necks.

"Here is where we boil the wine. It must heat to 212 degrees Fahrenheit for fourteen hours."

While Mallory discreetly dabbed at the sweat beading her upper lip, her host pointed to the tubes coiling from the necks of the copper pots.

"And there is where we capture the vapors that become Calvados. We boil seven hundred gallons of wine, yes? From that we get two hundred gallons of *eau de vie.*"

She understood the goal was to capture only the purest of the vapor, but she lost him when he tried to explain the difference between the heart, tailings and heads. The end product was a clear, amber liquid that was then stored for two to four years in Limousin oak casks inside caves cut into the hillside behind the distillery.

The potent fumes inside the caves were starting to get to Mallory by the time they emerged into the sunshine. The fresh air cleared her head enough to nod and smile when Monsieur Villieu insisted his visitors join him and his wife for lunch at a table set under an ancient oak tree.

As scarecrow-thin as her husband, Madame Villieu heaped bowls and plates for her guests before doing the same for herself and her husband. Her English was as spotty as Mallory's French, but the banquet she set out crossed all language barriers. A tureen of potato soup was followed by *salade Niçoise* and gargantuan platters of tomatoes, cheese, spicy sausage and sliced mutton. Following their host's lead, Mallory and Cutter slapped slab upon slab of meat, tomatoes and cheese onto fresh-baked baguettes.

In the midst of the feast, Monsieur Villieu poured stiff shots of his award-winning Calvados. "For *le trou Normand*, yes?"

"The Norman hole?" Mallory translated dubiously.

"Oui," he beamed. "We Normans have the long tradition. We drink Calvados in the middle of a meal such as this. It makes the hole, you understand, for more food to follow."

Tipping his head, he tossed back the brandy and thumped his glass on the table. His wife did the same.

"Now you," he urged.

Mallory glanced at Cutter, caught his grin, and raised her glass. *"Le trou Normand."*

"Le trou Normand," he echoed.

The Calvados slid down her throat like buttery apple cider. She tasted a hint of vanilla and rum raisin and started to smack her lips. Then the brandy hit her belly.

"Whoa!" Breathing fire, she fanned the air and regarded her empty shot glass with awe. "That is some potent stuff!"

Delighted by her pronouncement, Monsieur Villieu waved aside her protests and filled her glass again. She sipped cautiously this time and still had most of the brandy left when Cutter and his host excused themselves to talk business.

The women tried to converse during their absence. After a few moments of labored conversation, Madame Villieu got up to clear the table. Mallory helped by toting the tureen into the stone farmhouse that had probably stood on this site as long as the gnarled fruit trees and twisted vines.

They had the table cleared when the men returned. Their negotiations must have gone well, Mallory mused. Monsieur Villieu practically skipped across the lawn and Cutter wore a satisfied smile.

Feeling *extremely* mellow from the sunshine, good food and fine brandy, Mallory accepted the gift of a bottle of Monsieur Villieu's best before bidding her host and hostess goodbye and climbing into the car.

Cutter followed a different route back to the château, one that wound away from the coast. As she had the day before, Mallory found herself gazing across vast orchards. Now, however, she nursed a new appreciation for the apples of lower Normandy. Her head lolled against the seat. The breeze teased her hair.

Her mellow feeling dissipated somewhat when she noticed the time, but she couldn't bring herself to regret a whole day spent roaming the French countryside…especially with a companion as relaxed and easygoing as Cutter.

* * *

The château welcomed them home with windows gleaming gold in the afternoon sun and the roar of the sea loud against its cliffs. When Cutter pulled into the courtyard and came around to help her out, Mallory felt the sizzle again. It was there, arcing through the crisp fall air, tingling from the touch of his skin against hers.

Her breath snagged. Her eyes locked with his. She couldn't read the message in their cool gray depths, but she knew with everything female in her that Cutter had felt the heat, too.

Now, what the heck would they do about it?

The question was front and center in her mind as she returned Gilbért's greeting and followed him inside. Halfway down the long hall, she spotted a folded newspaper lying atop a stack of mail. The newspaper was French and local, but the black-and-white picture on the front page stopped her in her tracks.

Chapter 7

When Mallory came to an abrupt stop, Cutter was only a couple of paces behind her. He took a quick sidestep to avoid a collision while Gilbért turned in surprise at her involuntary groan.

"Oh, *nooo!*"

The fuzzy warmth engendered by her day in the sun and the hours spent with Cutter evaporated on the spot. Her insides twisting, Mallory pointed to the newspaper lying atop the hall table.

"It's him."

The newspaper showed only a partial head-and-shoulders shot, just enough for her to identify the man who'd accosted her yesterday at Mont St. Michel. That was enough. She knew with absolute certainty that when she unfolded the newspaper, her photo would appear beside his.

He must have seen her car float away and mouthed off to the people around him about the owner. Having such a notorious American lose her vehicle to the tides would make for a nice local news splash.

Gilbért glanced at the photo before politely handing her the paper. "You know this man, mademoiselle?"

"No, not really. I, uh, bumped into him yesterday at Mont St. Michel."

"It is *tragique,* how he dies."

"He's dead?"

"But yes. He falls down the stairs, there on the island."

Shocked, Mallory whipped open the folded paper. No mug shot of her, thank God, but the words *American* and *mort* leaped out from the caption below the photo.

The recently deceased had been loud and boorish and uncouth. Mallory felt no particular regret at his demise, only surprise and a guilty relief that her name hadn't been paired with his.

"I guess that's what happens when you combine steep steps and too much wine," she commented.

"Guess so," Cutter replied from just behind her.

His odd inflection brought Mallory's head around.

Disconcerted, she found his cool gray eyes narrowed on her instead of the photo.

"Hey, don't look at me. I didn't push him down any stairs, although I might have been tempted to if he'd pawed me one more time. In fact…"

Her joking tone faded. Brows drawing together, she glanced from Cutter to the photo and back again.

"In fact," she said slowly, "the last time I saw the man, you were holding his head under water."

Shrugging, Cutter disclaimed all responsibility. "He was still in the horse trough, swearing a blue streak when I left him. Too bad the dunking didn't sober him up."

Mallory's sudden and very uncomfortable pinprick of doubt faded. She'd spent more than twenty-four hours in Cutter Smith's company now. She couldn't remember the last time she'd felt so relaxed around—or been so attracted to—a man with his charm and rugged masculinity.

It was the comfort level that made her dismiss her momentary doubt as ridiculous…and the attraction that kept her lingering in the hall after Gilbért had confirmed they'd dine in that evening and departed in his slow, stately tread.

"About yesterday, when this guy grabbed me…"

She saw the question in his eyes. He had to be wondering where she was going.

"Yes?"

"I, uh, could have been more grateful when you came to my rescue."

"I wasn't looking for gratitude."

"I know." Remembering how she'd had to force a single, grudging word of thanks, Mallory grimaced. "It's just that… Well… I've become a little gun-shy around men lately."

Not to mention curt, suspicious and distrustful. She could do better. And Cutter certainly deserved better. He didn't know it, but he'd given her an incredible gift today. The relaxing hours in his company, the lunch under the trees, the long drive in the sunlight, had loosened the anger that had tied her in such tight knots these past weeks.

"Does that include me?" Cutter asked, hooking a brow.

"Not any more." The smile in her eyes matched the one in her heart. "Thanks for today, Monsieur Smith. I had a wonderful time. Calvados will be my brandy of choice from now on."

Mallory lifted a hand, aching to curve it over his cheek, but the no-grope rule worked both ways. She'd filed sexual harassment charges against a powerful legislator for inappropriate touching. In the process, she'd destroyed both her career and the warm spontaneity that had once been an integral part of her. The old Mallory might have completed the contact. The new Mallory hesitated.

This time, though, the urge to touch was reciprocal. She could sense it with everything that was female in her. Still, she hesitated, too scarred by the ugliness of the past months to follow through. She'd collected almost as many wounds as Cutter, she realized with a catch in her throat, except hers were on the inside.

Her hovering hand had started to drop when he resolved the matter by simply leaning forward. The warm skin of his cheek connected with her palm. His breath mingled with hers. She lifted her gaze, felt her pulse stutter.

Cutter's body reacted to the unspoken invitation even as his mind shouted at him to break the contact and back away.

Now!

She was his target, for God's sake! A possible traitor, intending to sell data that could do irreparable harm to her country. He'd played this game once, had ignored his instincts and fallen for a woman who'd damned near killed him—literally. It had taken long, painful months to recover from that fiasco.

Problem was, his instincts worked against his intellect this time. Common sense said to back off, but his gut said Mallory Dawes had no knowledge of the disk planted in her suitcase.

Cutter went with his gut.

Bending, he covered her mouth with his. He kept

the contact light, the kiss gentle. This was her show. He'd let her take it wherever she wanted it to go.

Okay, maybe a perverse corner of his mind was waiting to see if the stories about her were true, if she was as hot and hungry as her lovers had suggested.

If so, she had her hunger under control. His, on the other hand, bit into him with unexpected ferocity. His entire body protested when she broke the kiss and stepped back.

"I, ah, better go make some calls."

Cutter had to clench his fists to keep from reaching for her again. "I'll see you at dinner."

"Mmm. Hopefully, I'll have some good news about my various lost possessions by then and we can make it a farewell celebration."

"Hopefully," he agreed, still battling the ridiculous urge to drag her against him and take another taste of those soft, warm lips. He didn't breathe easy until she'd mounted the stairs and disappeared into her room.

Madame Picard had raided her employer's closet again. A long, multitiered skirt lay atop Mallory's bed, shimmering in a rainbow of rich jewel tones. Next to it was a short, boxy jean jacket trimmed with lace and sparkling crystals. The slip-on mules were also done in denim and lace and pouffy peacock feathers that ruffled in the sea breeze drifting through the windows.

Stroking the soft feathers, Mallory tried to picture Cutter's face when she glided into the petite dining salon decked out in Yvette's finery. Would she see the same hunger she'd glimpsed in his eyes a few moments ago? If she did, what would she do about it?

She knew darn well what she *wouldn't* do. She wouldn't back away after a mere brush of her mouth against his. Her pulse was still skittering from the kiss. She wanted more from Cutter Smith than one kiss, she acknowledged. Much more.

Her heart thumping at the thought, she blew softly on the peacock feathers. To heck with the legal bills still piled up at home. Before she left France, Mallory vowed, she'd treat herself to a pair of Yvette d'March- and originals. She darn well deserved them. Assuming American Express came through for her, that is.

Setting aside the mules, she scrounged in her purse for her list of telephone numbers and seated herself at the desk in the sitting room. The first call had her tapping her foot. The second came close to shredding her temper. By the third, she was gritting her teeth.

"Excuse me, but I did exactly as you requested. I had a notary witness my signature and faxed you his stamped certification. What more do you need to reimburse me for the lost checks?"

She gripped the receiver, quietly seething. She knew it wouldn't do any good to lose her temper, but she could feel it oozing through her fingers like slimy dough. When the officious clerk at the other end of the line indicated that he needed yet another level of approval before reimbursing her, Mallory asked to speak to his supervisor. The woman who came on was calm and apologetic.

"I'm so sorry this is taking so long, Miss Dawes, but there's a flag on your account."

Mallory counted to ten. "I'm sure there is. I lost my traveler's checks."

"Yes, I know, but…"

"But what?"

She heard the sound of a keyboard clicking.

"I really don't understand the hold," the supervisor said after a moment. "I'll research it and get back to you. I'm sure we'll resolve the matter soon."

"How soon is soon?"

"By tomorrow, hopefully. We have the cell phone number you gave us, also the number where you're staying. We'll contact you as soon as we obtain approval to release the funds."

Mallory resisted slamming down the phone—barely!—but her jaw was locked as she dialed the American Consulate. It remained tight all through the runaround she got from the Foreign Service officer.

Disgusted, she thudded the phone into its cradle and started to push away from the desk. Desperation convinced her to make one last try. With a mental note to reimburse her hostess for all these calls, she dialed the country code for the United States followed by Dillon Porter's private number at the Rayburn House Office Building.

She wasn't surprised when she got a recording. It was midmorning back home, and Dillon attended as many meetings as Congressman Kent. Chewing on her lower lip, Mallory waited for her former coworker's voice mail to end in a loud beep.

"Dillon, it's Mallory. I'm in France. Wish I could say I'm having a great time. Unfortunately, I lost my passport and can't seem to get hold of the right person at the American Consulate in Paris to authorize a temporary replacement. I'm getting a first class runaround."

No need to go into detail about everything else she'd lost. The sorry tale of riptides and sunken Peugeots would only make her sound as stupid as she felt.

"I know it's a lot to ask, but would you pull a few strings at State for me? Please?"

She cringed inwardly at the irony of her request. She'd accused Kent of sexual impropriety and left his employment in a huff. Now here she was, asking his senior staffer to throw her former boss's name around on her behalf.

"I'd appreciate anything you can do. Here's the number where I'm staying until I get this mess sorted out."

She rattled off the number, repeated it more

slowly, and hung up. After that, there was nothing to do but fill the tub with perfumed bubbles and soak away the irritation generated by the calls.

The bubbles helped. So did the elegant skirt, lace-trimmed jacket and feathery mules. But it was the sight of her dinner companion in his tailored slacks, silky black turtleneck and a rust-colored suede sport coat that put the glow back in her day. He was waiting for her at the bottom of the stairs, an elbow resting on the carved newel post.

"Madame Picard insists her veal Normandie can only be properly appreciated if eaten in the right setting. I've been sent to escort you to the main dining salon."

He crooked an elbow, and Mallory slid her arm through his. The suede felt buttery soft under her fingertips. The flesh beneath it was hard and smooth. Heat transferred from the material to her palm as he led her into the dining room.

The two place settings should have looked lonely all by themselves at the far end of the long banquet table. But candles, sparkling crystal and a tall spray of blood-red gladioli in a porcelain vase created a small island of elegance.

"Are we celebrating?"

The question jerked Mallory from her contemplation of the play of sinuous, suede-covered muscle.

"Huh?"

"You said when you went upstairs that you were going to make some calls and, hopefully, be ready for a farewell celebration at dinner. Do we pop a cork?"

"No. Everything is still a tangled mess."

She had to work to keep her spirits from taking another dive as Gilbért came forward to seat her in one of the throne-like chairs. She was wearing Yvette d'Marchand, Mallory lectured herself sternly. Basking in the glow of Limoges chandeliers. About to chow down with a man whose kindness was steadily chipping away at her unflattering opinion of the male of the species.

She continued the self-lecture while Gilbért set out a tray of antipasto and prepared an aperitif tableside. The elaborate ritual involved drizzling water through a slotted spoon holding a sugar cube. The water infused an anise-flavored liqueur called pastis and slowly turned the cloudy yellow liquid an opaque white.

Pouring the drinks into tall glasses, Gilbért presented them with a flourish. *"Voila."*

"Merci."

Mallory had learned her lesson with the apple brandy. She took only a few cautious sips, savoring the licorice tang that enhanced the flavors of the olives and prosciutto-wrapped melon slices.

"Care to give me a status report?" Cutter asked

when Gilbért had left them to enjoy their aperitifs. "Maybe I can help with the untangling."

"The status quo hasn't changed. The rental-car agency is still dithering over liability, American Express says there's a flag on my account, and you wouldn't believe the runaround I got from the U.S. Consulate. I called a friend back home who has some pull with the State Department. He should be able to help."

She tried for a Gallic shrug and was pretty proud of its nonchalance until the import of what she'd just said pierced her breezy facade. Like a backhanded slap, it wiped the smile from her face and knocked the breath from her lungs. Her eyes huge, she stared at Cutter in mounting dismay.

"Mallory?" Frowning, he set aside his glass. "What is it? What's the matter?"

"I—I just realized… The bureaucratic run-around… All these delays…" She could barely breathe. Swiping her tongue over suddenly dry lips, she croaked out an anguished whisper. "They may be deliberate."

Cutter went still. She wasn't surprised at the wary look that leaped into his eyes. He had to be wondering just what the heck he'd gotten himself into.

"What makes you think they're deliberate?" he asked with a cool edge to his voice.

She had to tell him. Much as it killed her, she had to hang the dirty linen out for him to see.

"I caused a stink back in the States, one that involved a very influential man. I wouldn't put it past him to retaliate by having one of his pals at the State Department label me in the system as a troublemaker, or worse."

Mallory couldn't believe it hadn't occurred to her before this moment. Like an idiot, she'd asked Dillon to drop his boss's name and pull a few strings without once considering that Congressman Kent could pull a whole bunch more. He hadn't spent twenty-plus years in Congress without building a wide circle of cronies who owed him favors.

"That's how they play the game in Washington," she said, struggling to keep the bitterness out of her voice. "You scratch my back, I'll scratch whatever portion of your anatomy you point in my direction."

Cutter regarded her for several silent moments. She could only imagine what he was thinking.

"Why don't you tell me who you crossed and how?" he said slowly.

"My former boss, Congressman Ashton Kent."

His lips pursed in a soundless whistle. Hers twisted in a wry grimace.

"I know, I know. Nothing like pitting yourself against one of the most powerful men in the United States."

"What happened?"

"Kent grabbed my ass once too often, so I filed a sexual harassment complaint."

Blowing out a ragged breath, Mallory stripped weeks of torment down to the sordid basics.

"Kent claimed I dressed too provocatively. That I left the top buttons of my blouse undone to entice him. He even produced a picture of the two of us, taken shortly after I joined his staff. There I was, smiling up at him in what he asserted was an open invitation."

Try as she might, Mallory couldn't hold back the tortuous doubts. They swamped her now, as they had so many times in the past weeks.

"I admired the man, Cutter! At first, anyway. Ashton Kent is a living legend in American politics. I was pretty jazzed to be asked to join his staff and probably didn't hold back when I was with him those first few weeks."

She cringed now at the memory of her initial, awestruck admiration for the silver-maned legislator. Maybe she *had* flirted a little. Maybe her eagerness to be considered a team player *could* have been interpreted as a come-on.

Then there was that business with her blouse.

"We were working late on draft legislation," Mallory related. "I'd slipped off my suit jacket. I didn't notice the top button on my blouse had come undone until Congressman Kent leaned over my shoulder and got an eyeful. That was the first time he fondled me."

Cutter said nothing, for which Mallory was profoundly grateful. The telling was difficult enough without editorial commentary.

"I was as surprised as I was embarrassed, but made it clear I wasn't interested. That's when the congressman informed me that I hadn't been hired for my brains."

Her listener broke his silence then. The pithy, one-syllable oath eased the tight knot in Mallory's chest.

"That's pretty much what I thought, too. So the second time Kent grabbed me, I filed a complaint. What followed wasn't pretty."

"No," Cutter growled, "I would imagine it wasn't."

She slumped against her chair back, relieved she didn't have to hide her dirty little secret from him any longer. "I'm surprised you didn't recognize me. My face, my personal history and detailed accounts of my sexual proclivities made just about every paper in the country."

"I travel a lot." His glance softened as it swept over her. "I'm guessing the media were a lot harder on you than they were on the congressman."

"You got that right. He came out looking like the poster boy for Viagra. I was painted as the promiscuous slut who tempted the poor man to sin."

Her dinner companion snorted. "Who in their right mind would believe Kent was a helpless victim?"

"His wife, for one. The arbitrator, for another.

And a dozen or so jerks like the one who hit on me at Mont St. Michel, all convinced Mallory Dawes was good for some raunchy, no-holds-barred sex."

Cutter toyed with his aperitif glass. He had strong hands, she thought, big and blunt-fingered.

"You sure that's why that guy hit on you?"

"I'm sure."

"He didn't just spot a beautiful woman sitting by herself and forget his manners?"

"Thanks for the compliment. God knows, I wish that was all it was. He made it clear, though, that he recognized me from the news stories and fully expected me to live up—or down—to my reputation."

She shrugged, feeling fifty pounds lighter now that she'd unburdened herself. "Sorry, Cutter. I guess I should have warned you that you were hooking up with the next best thing to a porn star."

She didn't expect the laughter that rumbled around in his chest. His gray eyes invited her to share in the joke.

"I didn't know there was a next best thing," he commented, grinning.

An answering chuckle gurgled up, surprising Mallory. She couldn't believe she was actually trading jokes about the degrading incident that had left a permanent stain on her psyche.

Okay, maybe not so permanent. The blot seemed to lighten a little more with each hour spent in Cutter's company. She was searching for a way to express her gratitude when Gilbért returned and held the door open for his wife to roll in a heavily laden cart.

The antipasto tray was whisked away. Wine goblets replaced the pastis glasses. Domes came off an array of silver serving dishes. With a beaming smile for his wife, the majordomo presented a platter garnished with parsley and cleverly carved lemon swans.

"I give you *le veau de la Normandie*."

Chapter 8

Mallory's account of her run-in with Congressman Kent gave Cutter a good deal more to chew on than Madame Picard's succulent veal.

Her account, brief as it was, tallied with the detailed summary in the background dossier OMEGA had put together on the Kent incident. She hadn't tried to gloss things over or minimize her part in the mess. If anything, she seemed to take a disproportionate share of the blame, and that left Cutter quietly seething.

He'd crossed paths with Ashton Kent. Twice. Once while Cutter was still in uniform and Kent had been part of a Congressional junket touring the Middle East. Again at Nick Jensen's high-priced D.C. restaurant, when Kent had disappeared into one of the private rooms with the well-endowed widow of a wealthy campaign contributor. Both times the old goat had struck Cutter as a walking, talking prick.

He didn't doubt for a minute Kent had felt up his bright-eyed new staffer. What really pissed Cutter off was that Mallory appeared to have taken most of the heat for it.

Had that made her bitter enough to walk away with a disk containing personal financial data belonging to millions of government workers, up to and including the President of the United States?

No way in hell!

His conviction grew firmer by the hour. Problem was, it was still based more on gut feeling than fact. He needed something definitive to eliminate her as anything more than a possible unwitting courier.

He waited until they'd finished dinner and agreed to Gilbért's suggestion they take coffee and dessert in the conservatory before steering the conversation back to the subject of retribution.

"So you think Kent may be retaliating against you by asking a pal to hold up your replacement passport?"

"I think it's a distinct possibility."

"How would he know you lost it in the first place?"

"Good question."

Mallory drifted to the tall windows, her gaze on the moonlit seascape outside. Cutter did his best to ignore the play of light and shadow on her profile as she scrunched her forehead and considered the possibilities.

"Maybe the State Department contacted my place of employment to verify my identity before issuing a temporary passport. Or maybe," she said slowly, "the contact came from American Express. They said there was a flag on my account. Congressman Kent chairs the House Committee on Banking and Trade. He exerts tremendous influence over the entire industry. He also works closely with NSA and Homeland Defense. I wouldn't put it past him to have flagged the financial records of everyone on his staff. Maybe everyone on the Hill. All in the name of national security."

"He wields that kind of power?" Cutter asked with a carefully manufactured blend of curiosity and outrage. "What happened to our right to privacy?"

The answer came swiftly and without the least hesitation.

"9/11."

Abandoning the moon-washed cliffs outside, Mallory turned and jammed her hands in the pockets of her lace-trimmed jacket.

"We're at war. An undeclared war, some argue, but everyone agrees that it threatens all Americans. Desperate times call for desperate measures. By following the money trail across international borders, we've located countless Al Qaeda cells and their financiers."

He didn't miss the collective *we*—or that Mallory Dawes identified with the good guys.

"I can't speak for anyone else," she continued, "but I'm more than willing to let Uncle Sam peek into my personal financial dealings if it will help take down bin Laden and his thugs."

Cutter and the rest of the OMEGA operatives served in the front lines in the war against terror. Personally, he didn't give a rat's ass about the rights of a suspected suicide bomber. Professionally, he'd respect those rights for the simple reason that violating them might screw the case against the suspect. He made no comment, however, until Mallory came off her soapbox with a look of embarrassed chagrin.

"I guess I'm just not real thrilled that Kent may be one of the ones doing the peeking."

"I can understand why."

As Cutter studied the moonlight dappling her upturned face, he had to admit there was something seriously wrong with this picture. Here they were, surrounded by the earthy perfume of the conservatory's potted palms, with stars studding the sky outside and the sea crashing against the cliffs below. His overwhelming urge was to take advantage of the exotic setting to kiss Ms. Dawes senseless. Instead, he was doing his damnedest to get her to incriminate herself. Grimly, he plowed ahead.

"Have you thought about getting back at Kent for all he's put you through? May still be putting you through?"

"God, yes!"

The vehemence sent a sudden chill through him, icing his veins. The rueful shrug that followed started a slow thaw.

"But I tried that once and failed dismally." She gave a small, self-deprecating laugh. "I can be pretty stubborn at times, but I'm not into self-flagellation or masochism. I decided before I left for France that I wasn't going to beat myself up over Congressman Ashton Kent any longer."

She slanted him a sideways glance and hesitated a moment before adding shyly, "You reinforced that decision, you know."

"Me? How?"

"By coming to my rescue the way you did. By giving me a glorious afternoon in the sun and two nights like this. But mostly, by reminding me not all men are like Kent."

Cutter's conscience started to squirm. He'd done exactly what he'd intended to do. Isolated the woman. Made her dependent on him. Gained her trust. So why the hell was he now feeling like a world-class heel?

"Don't pin a halo on me, Mallory. Kent and I have more in common than you think. You don't know how hard it was for me to keep my hands off you this afternoon."

"There's one significant difference," she said quietly. "I *want* your hands on me."

Sweating now, he was reminding himself of all the reasons why he shouldn't take her up on her starry-eyed invitation when she drifted closer.

"I liked touching you, Cutter."

He managed to resist until she dropped her gaze to his mouth.

"And I liked kissing you."

Well, hell! He'd never made any claims to being a saint. What's more, he'd given her fair warning.

Slamming the door on his conscience, he did what he'd ached to do earlier that afternoon. His arm snaked around her waist. His stance widened. Cradling her hips against his, he tunneled his free hand into her hair to hold her head steady and took what she offered.

The desire that had bitten into him earlier didn't compare to the hunger her eager mouth and hands now roused. Tightening his arm, he crushed her lips under his, as if daring her to unleash the beast.

Mallory slid her palms up the lapels of his jacket, felt his muscles straining under the suede, and surrendered to a rush of mindless pleasure.

This was the way it should happen. *This* was the way it was supposed to be. Desire feeding desire. Heat stroking heat. No politics. No sexual power plays. Only his mouth greedy on hers and her hands frantic to burrow through layers of fabric to get at the hard contours beneath.

She had to smother a curse when the rattle of wheels announced the arrival of Madame Picard and her serving cart. Cutter wasn't as restrained. With a muttered expletive, he released her and rolled his shoulders to settle his sport coat while Mallory tugged down the jacket that had ridden up over her hips.

They weren't quite quick enough. Madame Picard's glance went from one to the other as she rolled her cart across the tiles.

"You wish me to serve dessert?"

"That's okay," Cutter said, taking charge. "We'll serve ourselves."

With a smile and a small bow, madame departed. The interruption hadn't lasted more than a few seconds. Just long enough for reason to prevail…if either of them was inclined toward reason.

Mallory certainly wasn't. After so many weeks of doubting herself, of hiding behind sunglasses and avoiding men's glances, she reveled in the heat in Cutter's eyes when they whipped back to her. Her pulse skipping, she scooped a two-tiered plate from the cart.

"I've got the chocolate truffles and strawberries. You bring the whipped cream."

Dessert was the last thing on Cutter's mind as he snatched up the silver pot containing fresh, frothy cream. Visions of where and how he would spread the stuff damned near had him tripping over his own feet.

He maintained his balance and enough presence of mind to snag their unfinished bottle of wine from the cooler as he followed Mallory through the grand dining salon. Once they'd mounted the stairs and closed the door to her sitting room behind them, however, the bottle, silver pot and two-tiered plate were set aside and forgotten.

Mallory came into his arms with unrestrained eagerness. The ugly insinuations and allegations of promiscuity flashed through Cutter's mind, only to die an instant death the moment she went up on tiptoe and locked her arms around his neck. She gave as much as she took, but the giving was warm and generous, the taking anything but rapacious.

He was the one who yanked open the buttons of her jacket. *He* almost choked when he peeled down the denim and saw the lacy camisole beneath. *His* heart jackhammered against his chest when she angled her head and nibbled her way from his lower lip to his chin to his throat.

Cutter had to fight to keep from tossing her over his

shoulder and hauling her to the bed in the next room. The instincts she stirred in him were primitive, almost primeval. He couldn't remember the last time he'd wanted a woman as much as he wanted this one. Hell, he'd *never* wanted one as much as he did Mallory.

Not even the Danish beauty who'd arched and panted and hooked her legs around his waist only hours before she triggered the device that created such carnage and devastation.

The realization locked Cutter's jaw. He stepped back, fists balled, every muscle and tendon in his body raw with the memory.

"I'm so sorry." Stricken, Mallory touched a feather-light finger to the scars she'd just kissed. "I didn't think... I didn't realize... Do they still hurt you?"

They did, but not in the way she thought.

Cutter almost ended things then. He was pretty sure he would have, too, if she hadn't proceeded to yank the rug out from under his feet.

"I'm sorry," she whispered again, leaning forward to drop a tender kiss on the underside of his chin. "I'll be more gentle. I promise."

The irony of it hit before the absurdity. In her own words, she'd been publicly branded as the next thing to a whore. Yet she stood there with sympathy swimming in her big brown eyes, reining in her natural urges, promising to go easy on him.

On *him!*

His doubts sank out of sight. Insides turning to mush, he chuckled and tugged her against him.

"You just let rip, sweetheart. I'll do my best to grin and bear it."

All inclination toward laughter had disappeared by the time he scooped her up and carried her into the bedroom. So had any pretense that he was a passive player in the game. He was rock-hard and hurting when he dragged down the silken coverlet.

Stretching her out on the pale-blue sheets, he stripped off her lacy camisole and briefs. The need to possess her made his hands unsteady as he shed his own clothes, but he managed to fish a condom from his wallet.

A strangled sound came from the bed. Throwing a quick glance over his shoulder, he saw Mallory propped up on one elbow.

"What's that slogan?" she choked out as he joined her on sheets as soft as snow. "'Never leave home without them?' Reminds me of a certain financial institution that shall remain nameless at this… Oh!"

Cutter smiled at her breathless gasp and shifted his weight. They fitted together perfectly, her mouth within easy reach of his, her breasts flattened against his chest. He shifted a little more to the side and stroked his hand from her breasts to her belly and back again.

She was incredible, he thought while he could

still think at all. Her skin was smooth and creamy and flushed with heat. Her belly hollowed under his palm. The pale hair of her mound was soft and silky to his touch.

Cutter fully intended to draw out the foreplay as long as possible, priming her, testing his own limits. But when he found the slick flesh between her thighs, his mind shut down and his body took over. Fitting himself against her, he locked his mouth on hers and sank into her wet, welcoming heat.

They found a rhythm as old as time. Mallory's skin grew damp with sweat. Her nipples ached from Cutter's nipping, sucking kisses. She rolled atop him to return the favor and had contorted to work her way down to his chest when her entire body went taut.

She jerked upright. Hands, teeth and thighs clenched as her climax slammed into her. Wave after wave of pleasure ricocheted through her belly. She thought she heard Cutter groan. She knew his muscles bunched under her bottom just before he thrust upward.

She collapsed onto his chest seconds later. Or maybe it was hours. She didn't have a clue. The only reality that penetrated her sensual haze was the hammer of his heart under her ear.

Mallory floated slowly back to earth, vaguely aware of the cold air prickling her backside.

Flopping onto the mattress, she dragged up the tangled sheet and nuzzled into Cutter's side. She must have dozed a little before she came awake with the scent of their lovemaking teasing her nostrils. Burying her face in the angle between his neck and shoulder, she touched her lips to the warm skin.

"Mmm. You taste salty."

"I am salty. And thirsty." Easing his arm free, he leaned over her and dropped a kiss on her still-tender lips. "How about I retrieve the wine?"

"Great idea. Bring the other goodies, too." She scrambled upright and hooked the sheet under her arms. "We'll have our own private picnic."

Cutter did as asked. He brought the dessert tray and pot of still-frothy whipped cream first, then went back for the wine. Mallory had bitten into her second truffle when he returned.

"You are *not* going to believe how wonderful these are," she gushed. "The first one was mocha, flavored with Cointreau. This one is chocolate, hazelnut and rum. Here, take a bite."

Smacking her lips in exaggerated ecstasy, she offered him the remaining morsel. He bent to take it, but she didn't see her playful mood reflected in his expression. He'd turned thoughtful during his two trips into the sitting room.

Okay. All right. So he wasn't into postcoital picnics. No big deal.

She reached deep inside for something blasé to cover the awkward moment and came up empty. When he stood beside the bed and looked down at her, though, she knew the moment had stretched too thin to simply ignore.

"Is something wrong?"

He hesitated a few seconds too long.

"Wait," Mallory said, her heart sinking. "Don't tell me. I can guess. You're having a sudden attack of conscience."

She'd hit the mark. She could see it in his face. Dismayed, she shook her head.

"I should have known this little romantic interlude was too good to be true. That *you* were too good to be true."

"Mallory…"

"You're married, aren't you?"

"No."

"Engaged."

"No."

"In love with a twenty-two-year-old cowboy from Montana."

"What?"

If she hadn't been so mortified by his withdrawal, she might have derived immense satisfaction from his stunned expression.

"Hey, I saw *Brokeback Mountain*. I pretty much fell in love with Heath Ledger myself."

His mouth opened. Snapped shut. In a tone that sounded like glass grinding, he refuted her allegations.

"Did it feel like you were in bed with someone nursing a taste for twenty-something cowboys?"

"I don't know. Let me think about it for a minute."

"Oh, for…!"

Tangling a hand in her hair, he tugged her head back. His eyes weren't cool any longer, she noted.

"In case you haven't noticed, my taste runs to twenty-nine-year-old blondes who run around losing passports, sinking rental cars and smearing chocolate all over their lips."

When he proceeded to kiss away the aforementioned chocolate, Mallory's doubts subsided. Temporarily. Only after he broke the kiss to lick at the corner of her mouth did her thoughts reengage. Curious, she cocked her head.

"How did you know?"

"Know what?"

"How old I am. Was that just a lucky guess?"

"I must have overheard you give the information to the gendarme at Mont St. Michel."

"I don't remember giving my age," she said, a frown gathering. "My name, yes. And your cell phone number. Not my age."

Impatience flickered across his face as a sick feeling churned in the pit of Mallory's stomach.

"Oh, God! You knew."

Dragging the sheet with her, she scrambled to her feet. Strawberries and truffles spilled everywhere.

"You knew all about me, didn't you? You *did* read the papers, or saw the reports on TV. You knew about me, yet you sat there at the table and listened while I spilled my sad little tale."

He didn't try to deny it. He couldn't. The truth was stamped all over his face.

"Yes, I knew who you were."

Her chin lifted. She'd indulge in some serious self-flagellation and name-calling later. Right now she just wanted him gone before she burst into tears.

"Glad I gave you some fun, Mr. Smith. Now get out of my room."

"Listen, Mallory, I did know who you were, but…"

"But what?" she jeered. "You lied about not reading the news stories because you wanted to see if they were true? If I was hot as they said? Well, now you know. They're true. Every one of them."

"To hell they are."

"You can go home, sell the latest chapter in this squalid serial to the tabloids, make millions."

"Dammit, just listen a moment! I didn't see any TV specials or pore through the tabloids. I studied the dossier put together by the outfit I work for."

"You got a dossier?" Her face went slack with surprise before morphing into a full-fledged scowl. "On me?"

"Yes."

"Why? You're a wine broker, for pity's sake. Why would you…? Oh!"

Swirls of conversation came back to her. Reeling, she recalled how Cutter had cleverly pumped her for information about her job at the Department of Commerce.

"Oh, Lord! How much of an idiot can one person be? This has to do with my job at the International Trade Administration, doesn't it? What did you think you could get from me, Smith? Preferential status on ITA's market listing? Inside information on your foreign competition?"

Cutter came within a breath of telling her the truth then. *Not* because of his mounting guilt for taking advantage of her vulnerability. Or the odd, indefinable emotion that had jolted through him when she'd pressed her lips against his puckered flesh.

It wasn't love. He'd only known the woman for all of two days. People didn't fall in love that quickly, except maybe in movies. Like *Brokeback Mountain*.

Christ!

No, he wanted to level with her for purely professional reasons. Mallory Dawes didn't have any knowledge of the disk tucked in a pocket of her suitcase. Cutter would stake his reputation on that. Correction, he'd stake what was left of his reputation after pulling an 007 and hopping into bed with his target.

She might, however, be able to help him determine *how* the disk got into her suitcase. For that, he needed her full cooperation.

Before he could read her in on the situation, though, he had to clear it with OMEGA's director. Lightning trusted his agents' instincts, gave them complete authority in the field, but this particular op involved the President of the United States.

"Mallory, listen to me. Please."

He figured he had all of thirty seconds to convince her he didn't rank right up there with Congressman Kent as a total sleaze.

"I did receive a dossier on you, but it had nothing to do with the wine business or your job at the International Trade Administration. I can't explain what it *did* concern. Not yet. You'll have to trust me a little longer."

Her chin jutted. Fury put bright spots of red in her cheeks. "Give me one good reason why I should."

She had him there. Cutter didn't think she was in any mood to appreciate a reference to the hours they'd spent together. Or to the fact that they both still wore each other's scent on their skin. All he could do was curl a knuckle under her chin and tip her face to his.

"I can't give you one, sweetheart. But I will. As soon as I make some calls, I promise. Just trust me a little longer, okay?"

"I'll think about it." Her eyes stormy, she jerked away from his touch. "Now get out of my room."

Chapter 9

The coded signal came in just as Mike Callahan was about to turn the control desk over to his relief.

It was only a little past four in the afternoon, D.C. time, but it was late evening on the coast of Normandy. Mike had taken Slash's report several hours ago. He'd figured on grabbing a few hours sleep while his field operative did the same.

His pulse kicking up a notch at the unscheduled contact, Mike nudged his relief aside and brought Slash's digitized image up on the screen.

"Thought you were locked down for the night, buddy."

"I was. I am."

Sliding into his seat at the console, Mike noted the rigid set to Cutter's jaw. Someone or something had gotten to him.

"What's up?"

"I want to read Dawes in on the op."

"Roger that."

Callahan didn't question the abrupt change in plans. He trusted Cutter Smith's instincts implicitly. He should. The two of them went back a long way. Over the years they'd shared ops, beers and the occasional night out with whatever females they happened to be involved with at the time.

Those years had forged bonds that went beyond friendship. Danger had further hardened the bonds to tempered steel. On one memorable occasion, Slash had manned a Black Hawk helicopter's 20mm cannon to hold off more than fifty enraged rebels while Mike scrambled for the hoist cable that would extract him from the sweltering jungle. On another, Mike had jumped in a Navy jet and flown halfway across the world to accompany Slash on the agonizing medevac flight home after a certain traitorous bitch had left him bleeding, burned and unconscious.

Neither of them talked about that long, horrific flight. Or about the woman Cutter had later tracked down. Some things didn't need discussing. Reading a target into an operational mission with such top-level interest, however, did.

"I'll have to run this by Lightning."

"I know."

"He's going to want to know the rationale."

"Tell him…"

Slash's hesitation was as uncharacteristic as his scowl. Mike waited a beat, wondering what the hell had happened in the scant hours since his last report.

"Tell him I'm convinced Dawes didn't know the disk was in her suitcase. I want to work with her, see if she can shed some light on how it got there."

"You sure she'll cooperate? She might not take kindly to learning that you've had her in your sights all this time."

"She's already tipped to the fact that I have more than a friendly interest in her." He paused again, then added a gruff postscript. "Considerably more, as it happens. Things, uh, got personal tonight."

Mike had spent too many years undercover to react to that bit of news, but he had to work to hold back a low whistle. The only other time Cutter had led with his dick instead of his head, he'd wound up in a burn ward.

"You sure you know what you're doing, buddy?"

"Yeah, I'm sure." Cutter stared straight into the camera. "Get back with me as soon you talk to Lightning."

"Will do."

Mike didn't need to check the electronic status board to know Lightning wasn't on site. He'd departed some hours ago to participate in a charity sports event at the Army-Navy Country Club. Wearing his Presidential Envoy/millionaire restaurateur persona, Nick Jensen and his wife, OMEGA's chief of communications, were knocking tennis balls around the court at something like a thousand dollars a whack.

So was Nick's executive assistant, Mike remembered with a sudden kink in his gut. Gillian had called up to advise Control she'd be at the country club with Nick and Mackenzie.

"You've got the stick," Mike instructed his relief. "I don't want to catch Lightning in midswing and throw him off his game. I'll deliver Slash's request in person."

Shrugging into his red windbreaker with its Military Marksmanship Association patch on the breast pocket, he dug his car keys out of the pocket of his jeans and descended to the tunnel that led to OMEGA's specially shielded underground parking facility.

His tan Blazer sat in its usual spot. The vehicle was only two years old but had already logged over a hundred thousand miles. Mike knew it was good for another hundred-plus. Drew McDowell, code name Riever, owned and operated a chain of classic car restoration shops in his civilian life. Drew had personally replaced the rods and adjusted the timing. The Blazer could go from zero to sixty in three-point-six seconds.

The acceleration came in handy when Mike wasn't in the field, working an op for OMEGA, and had to eat up road between his Alexandria condo and the Firearms Training Unit at Quantico, where he taught agents from a half dozen federal agencies the fine art of blowing away bad guys.

The familiar stink of the solvent he used to clean his weapons after a shoot permeated the Blazer. Mike kept a complete kit in the rear well—bores, brushes, rods, gun vise, wood and metal polish—all the tools of his trade. He carried his Mauser 86sr in a concealed compartment, as well. NATO snipers trained with a military version of Mauser, which featured a ventilated stock to dissipate heat and a detachable box for quick switching from high- to low-penetration rounds. Mike's had been custom built to his specifications.

Exiting the garage, he opened the car windows and let the brisk September air blow away the stink. Fall was in full swing, he noted absently as he negotiated the pre-rush hour rush. The oak and chestnut trees had already begun to turn. Fat yellow mums nodded from pots and planters along Massachusetts Avenue. His eyes shielded from the bright sun by mirrored sunglasses, Mike cut over to the Theodore

Roosevelt Bridge to avoid the usual logjam on 395 and cruised along Memorial Parkway. As always, the solid bulk of the Pentagon stirred memories of his years in uniform.

His first months had been rough. He'd arrived at boot camp with a chip the size of Rhode Island on his shoulder and a mouth to match. It hadn't taken long for a lean, wiry DI to cut the new recruit down to size. By the time Mike graduated from boot camp, he'd found a home and the family he'd never had.

He'd started in law enforcement, a rookie cop with few skills except the ability to put every round dead center at the practice range. That skill had served him well after transferring to an ultra-secret, highly mobile Special Ops forward insertion unit.

Mike would still be in uniform if Nick Jensen hadn't convinced him he could serve his country just as effectively in a different capacity. The transition was a wrench, but Mike had never looked back. OMEGA was every bit as tight as his Special Ops unit.

And Nick Jensen made one helluva boss, he thought as he pulled up at the gatehouse of the hallowed Army-Navy Country Club, a scant mile south of the Pentagon. Two guards manned the gate, along with a civilian-type Mike immediately identified as Secret Service. Wondering which of the President's numerous progeny were participating in the tennis tournament, he flipped open the ID case that cleared him for access to any government installation.

With a respectful nod, the guard activated the wrought-iron gates. "Welcome to Army-Navy, sir."

"Thanks."

Tucking away his ID, Mike navigated the winding road that cut through the superbly manicured grounds. Founded in the early 1920s to provide recreational facilities for military and civilians assigned to the nation's capital, the sprawling complex covered more than five hundred acres of wooded Virginia countryside. Mike played an occasional round of golf at the club, but didn't go out of his way to rub elbows with the generals, admirals, senators and foreign ambassadors who made up the bulk of the membership.

The indoor/outdoor tennis courts were some way past the redbrick, white-pillared clubhouse. A festive crowd had gathered to watch the matches underway on all four outdoor courts. Cheers rose with every returned volley, while groans abounded after each missed shot.

Nick and Mackenzie were hard at it on court number three. Mike could see the sweat streaking his boss's dark-gold hair. Mac had drawn her mink-brown mane back in a ponytail that whipped from side to side with every strong-armed swing. They were matched with a hook-nosed reporter from the

Washington Post and his partner, an angular, gray-haired woman Mike recognized as an undersecretary of defense.

But it was the couple on court two that riveted Mike's attention. Gillian's blouse and thigh-skimming pleated skirt were both pristine white, but she'd topped them with a hot pink sleeveless V-neck sweater. Her sun visor was the same neon pink, trimmed with sparkling crystals. And when she stretched to return a killer serve, she flashed a glimpse of matching briefs.

Mike's throat went dry. He knew damned well tennis stars like Venus and Serena Williams were glamming up the courts with colorful outfits and sequined shoes. He just wasn't prepared for the sight of Gillian Ridgeway in pink panties with a crystal heart etched on the right butt cheek.

Or for her partner's reaction when she scored the winning point. Whooping with delight, the jerk caught her up and whirled in a full circle before planting a kiss on her laughing lips.

"Game, set and match to Ridgeway and Olmstead," the announcer intoned while Mike's eyes narrowed to slits behind his sunglasses.

The urge to smash his fist in this guy Olmstead's face was completely irrational. That didn't make it any less atavistic. Jaw tight, he jammed his hands in his pockets.

They were still there, bunched into tight fists, when Gillian gathered her gear and came off the court. She accepted the congratulations of several spectators before she spotted him off to the side of the crowd.

"Mike!"

A smile sparkled in her vivid blue eyes. A *friendly* smile, he lectured himself sternly, the kind she'd drop on any casual acquaintance.

"Did you see the match?"

"Only the last few minutes." Which would, he knew, replay repeatedly in his head for nights to come. "You're good."

"I'm okay. My golf game is better, though."

Dragging up one end of the towel draped around her neck, she daubed at the sweat plastering tendrils of her jet-black hair to her temples.

"I understand you've been known to hit the fairways," she commented. "Maybe we should get up a foursome some weekend. You and I could take on Uncle Nick and my father. Dad is always looking for fresh blood."

Mike couldn't think of anything that would throw off his concentration more completely than sharing a golf cart with Gillian Ridgeway while two of OMEGA's most lethal operatives watched their every move.

"Or I could pair up with Dayna," she suggested with a grin, referring to an OMEGA operative who just happened to be an Olympic gold medalist. "We girls could take on you boys."

He was still trying to adjust to being classified as a "boy" when Gillian's partner strolled up and draped an arm across her shoulders.

"Hey, Jilly. We need to sign the score sheet."

Mike had made a career in the profession of arms. He could bring up his weapon, fix a target in his crosshairs and squeeze off a shot in less time than it took other men to chamber a round. With the same split-second precision, he sized up Jilly's partner as arrogant, over-confident and possessive.

"In a minute." Looking too damned comfortable in the circle of the man's arm, Gillian made the introductions. "Wayland, this is Mike Callahan. Mike, Wayland Olmstead."

Mike knew the name and the rep, if not the face. Yale undergrad. Harvard law. Hotshot young attorney carving a niche for himself at the National Security Agency.

"Good to meet you, Callahan."

The grip went with the man. Too strong and too long, as if signaling his power. Mike resisted the impulse to crunch the jerk's knuckles.

"I see you're a shooter," Olmstead commented, eyeing the Military Marksmanship Association patch.

"Not *just* a shooter," Gillian corrected. "A world champion. Mike instructs at the Federal Law Enforcement Academy at Quantico," she added, supplying his civilian cover. "He's the man my father strong-armed into teaching me to shoot."

Adam Ridgeway was more than capable of teaching his daughter how to handle weapons. So was her mom, for that matter. Maggie Sinclair's exploits were still the stuff of legend at OMEGA. But both parents had preferred a professional instructor, insisting that Mike could be more objective in assessing Gillian's strengths and weaknesses. Shows what they knew.

"You did a heck of a job," Olmstead said, squeezing her shoulders. "Jilly knocks down more sporting clays than I do every time we take out the Blassingames."

The message was about as subtle as a rifle butt to the bridge of the nose. A used Blassingame, if you could find one, went for a cool fifty thousand.

Idiot.

"I think you should know," Gillian warned, her eyes twinkling. "Samantha and Tank have been pestering Dad for lessons, too."

Mike had no problem with teaching Jilly's college-aged sister to shoot, but the prospect of putting a gun into the hands of her teenaged brother drained every ounce of blood from his face.

Gillian had to laugh at his expression. He couldn't have looked more horrified if she'd shrugged off

Wayland's arm, gone up on tiptoe and given him a class-A liplock.

Something she'd thought about doing more and more frequently, she mused as a roar rose from the bleachers surrounding court three.

"Game, set and match to Jensen and Jensen."

"Good for Nick and Mackenzie!" With another squeeze, Wayland steered Gillian back toward the courts. "Let's go congratulate each other."

"Coming, Mike?"

"I'll wait here." He adjusted his sunglasses and gave her one of his Uncle-Mike-to-little-Jilly smiles. "Tell Nick I need to talk to him when he gets a minute."

One of these days, she vowed as she accompanied Wayland through the milling crowd, she'd have to convince him she was all grown up.

After consulting with Lightning, Mike waited until he was back in the Blazer to contact Cutter. Traffic was a bitch, crawling along like a snail on tranquilizers, belching diesel fumes into the slowly gathering dusk.

The traffic snarl matched Mike's mood. He could have gone all month without that glimpse of Olmstead tipping a champagne glass to Gillian's lips.

Hell, all year.

With a surly sneer for the unbroken stream of red taillights ahead, he punched a two-digit code into his phone.

"Lightning gave the green light," he relayed when Cutter's image appeared on the screen. "You can read Dawes into the op."

"Roger that."

The leap of satisfaction in Cutter's face had Mike biting back a warning. Slash knew what he was doing. He wouldn't fall for another female with a soul as flawed as the one who'd damned near killed him.

"When do you plan to tell her?"

"First thing in the morning."

"Good luck."

"Thanks, Hawk."

Cutter woke early the next morning.

A cold wind rattled the windows, causing the château to creak and groan with the prerogative of age, but he didn't hear a sound from the suite next door.

That was fine with him. He needed a good run to clear his head. He'd lost several hours of sleep to the image of Mallory's angry face and stormy eyes when she jerked away from his touch. Even more to the vivid memory of her slick flesh and low, throaty moan when she'd climaxed in his arms. He'd have to talk hard and fast to recover the ground he'd lost last night. Faster still to get her into bed again.

With various strategies for how he'd break the

news that she was the primary suspect in an identity
theft of massive proportions kicking around in his
head, Cutter pulled on the jogging suit OMEGA's
Field Dress Unit had included in his hastily assembled kit. He would have preferred his usual Nikes and
well-worn gray sweats but had to admit the choco-
late-brown velour designer job felt as soft as a fuzzy
kitten against his skin.

He followed the scent of fresh-brewed coffee and
rising yeast to a kitchen aglow with copper pots.
Gilbért was seated at a peg-and-board oak table with
his jacket hooked on the back of his chair and the
remains of his breakfast in front of him. Madame
Picard stood at a granite slab of a counter and rolled
pastry dough with floured arms.

"'Morning."

Abashed to be caught in his shirtsleeves, Gilbért
scrambled for his jacket. *"Excusez-moi,* monsieur. I
did not hear the bell."

"I didn't ring. Please, sit down. I just want some
coffee before I head out for a run. May I join you?"

"But of course."

The coffee was thick and tarry black, the cream
light and frothy. One cup led to another, then to a
brioche fresh from the oven. Regretfully, Cutter
passed on a second until after his run.

The morning mist swirled gray and thick when
Gilbért disarmed the security system and Cutter

exited into the cobbled courtyard. Discreetly placed cameras tracked his progress through the gate and onto the long, sweeping drive.

Instead of following the drive to the main road, he opted for a path that led along the cliffs. A mile at a slow trot loosened muscles that hadn't been exercised in several days. With the ocean hidden by the fog but roaring loudly in his ears, Cutter gradually lengthened his stride. Salty mist dewed on his face. Damp air filled his lungs. Thoughts of Mallory Dawes looped through his head.

Six miles later, the velour was drenched with sweat and Cutter had decided on a direct approach. He wouldn't gain anything by pussyfooting around the issue. First he'd shower and shave. Then he'd tell Mallory about the disk, inform her that he'd had her under close surveillance since Paris, and brace himself for the firestorm that would follow.

He accomplished the first two items on his agenda with minimum fuss and maximum speed.

His cheeks tingling from the rapid scrape of his razor, he tugged on slacks and a lightweight knit sweater in a peacocky blue, compliments of Field Dress, and rapped on the door to Mallory's suite. When she didn't answer, he tried the small dining salon, the oak-paneled library and the music room before once again making his way to the kitchen.

Madame Picard was still at the counter, peeling apples for the pie shell she'd baked while he was running.

"The run?" she inquired politely. "It is good?"

"Very good. Has Mademoiselle Dawes come down?"

"Oui." The paring knife made a small circle in the air. "She comes, she goes."

"Goes?"

"Oui. The telephone rings, and mademoiselle, she asks Gilbért to drive her."

"Drive her where?"

"Into town, to the train station."

Cutter smothered a vicious oath. "How long?"

"Pardon?"

"How long have they been gone?"

Her shoulders lifted in that quintessential Gallic shrug. "Five minutes, perhaps ten."

Cutter spun on his heel and sprinted for the stairs to retrieve his car keys, cursing all the way.

Chapter 10

Mallory stared unseeing at the mist-shrouded pines drifting past the windows of Madame d'Marchand's Rolls Royce Silver Cloud. Beside her, Gilbért hummed to himself as he steered through the forest that edged right down to the cliffs on this stretch of coast.

She should have been feeling like a princess. After all, she'd spent the past two nights in a castle and was now being conveyed to town in a chrome-laden behemoth that glided along with slow, ponderous grace. Instead, she wanted to bite something. Or someone.

She supposed she should thank Cutter for waiting until last night to bring the walls of her fairy-tale castle tumbling down around her. At least she'd got to spend a whole day roaming the French country-side, lazing in the sun, sipping apple brandy. An evening filled with sparkling crystal and *le veau de la Normandie.* And let's not forget that hot, sweaty session between the sheets.

She ground her teeth, and Gilbért raised an in-quiring brow.

"Yes, mademoiselle?"

Shifting in her seat, Mallory glanced at the stately majordomo. He appeared so calm, so dignified, with his salt-and-pepper hair, neatly trimmed mustache and spiffy tweed driving cap.

"Mademoiselle is disturbed?" he asked, unbend-ing enough to tip her a look of friendly concern.

She started to deny it. Shielding her thoughts and emotions had become a necessary survival mechan-ism over the past months. She was feeling just raw enough, though, to blow a long huff of self-disgust.

"Did you ever make a fool of yourself over someone? A total, twenty-four-carat fool?"

"But of course. I am French. It is required."

"Wish I could use nationality as my excuse," Mallory said glumly. "With me, it's just plain stupidity."

"What is life without such folly, eh?" His lips curving, Gilbért relaxed his gloved hands on the steering wheel. "Madame Picard was the belle of our village. All the men puff their chests and strut like the peacock when she strolls by. She tortures me, *ma petite Jeanette,* until I go mad with despair and decide to drown myself in the village well. It is a gesture, you understand, a foolish gesture. I have gone down the well many times as a boy, but now I am too big and become stuck. It takes a team of horses to pull me out, while the whole village watches. We laugh about it still, Madame Picard and I."

Gilbért's rich chuckle invited Mallory to share in the absurdity of life in general and love in particular.

Okay, she thought, smiling at his tale, so maybe she wasn't the only woman in history to fall for a sexy smile and a body to match. Throw in a propensity to appear just when a girl needed him most and a seemingly sympathetic ear, and it was no wonder she'd let desire cloud her judgment where Cutter Smith was concerned.

The stupid thing was, deep down inside she still wanted to trust him. Against all reason, despite every bitter lesson she'd learned in recent months, she wanted to give him the time he'd asked for. How stupid was that?

She was squirming inwardly at the answer when a figure darted out of the forest. Planting himself in the middle of the road, he waved his hands above his head and signaled for them to stop.

With a low grunt, Gilbért stomped on the brakes. His eyes narrowed under the brim of his tweed cap.

"I know this one. He is the son of the baker in town."

Judging by the curl to Gilbért's lip, he didn't hold the baker's son in particularly high esteem. Mallory's glance cut back to the man on the road.

Skinny and spike-haired, he looked to be in his early twenties. His jeans were fashionably ragged, showing large patches of bare skin. His jacket was also denim. The black T-shirt he wore underneath sported a heart skewered by a stiletto dripping blood.

"Wait in the car, mademoiselle." Gilbért put his shoulder to the Rolls' heavy door. "I will see what he wants."

Whatever it was led to an escalating exchange of words and gestures. Mouths twisted into sneers. Arms were flung. Chins were flipped. When the kid dragged an arm across his nose to wipe it, an obviously disgusted Gilbért turned and stalked toward the car.

Before he'd taken more than a few steps, the baker's son whipped something out from under his jacket. Mallory caught only a glint of metal before he raised his arm and brought it down on Gilbért's skull. The older man crumpled like an old suit of clothes.

"Hey!"

Mallory was out of the car before Gilbért hit the ground. The kid spun toward her, clutching what she now saw was a small but lethal-looking revolver.

She froze, her breath thick in her throat, as he let loose with a torrent of French. The volume rose with each agitated phrase, until he was almost shouting at her.

"I don't understand." Her voice cracked. Her mind fought to find the right translation. *Je, uh, ne comprend...*"

"I will have it!"

"Have what?"

"Everything. The purse. The wallet. What you carry in the car."

Drugs, she thought when her brain unfroze enough to register anything except the gun barrel aimed at her midsection. The wild eyes. The runny nose. He had to be on drugs. Only someone really messed up in the head would risk a robbery in broad daylight with a man who could easily identify him lying in the dirt at his feet.

The realization she was facing an armed junkie would have scared the crap out of her if a second realization hadn't hit right on top of that one. *Because* the man lying in the dirt at this guy's feet could identify him, he might not be inclined to leave either Gilbért or Mallory behind as witnesses.

"The purse," the kid shouted, his gun shaking with the effort. "Throw it down, in the road. Then move away from the car."

Struggling desperately to recall the tips imparted in her self-defense course, Mallory tugged at the strap of the purse draped across her chest and one shoulder. Most of the advice had to do with avoiding dangerous situations. Never pick up hitchhikers. Stick to well-lighted areas. Travel in pairs.

The options narrowed down considerably when confronted by an armed robber. Don't resist. That was rule one. Her life was more valuable than her possessions. Except in this case, she didn't have many possessions and she couldn't shake the sick certainty that her life hung by a very thin thread with this guy.

Rule two, don't make any sudden moves that might make the attacker think she was reaching for a concealed weapon. Dear God, what she wouldn't give for a concealed weapon!

Rule three… Do whatever you could to get away if he tried to force you into the car and run like hell in a zigzagging pattern.

Her hand shaking, Mallory dragged her purse over her head. She could zigzag it into the trees lining the road. Maybe. If she ran, though, she'd leave Gilbért at the mercy of this crackhead.

"Here." Her mind racing in frantic circles, she dangled the purse. "This is all I have. Just take it, okay?"

"Throw it down onto the road and move away from the car."

She tossed the purse, but not onto the pavement. With a twitchy jerk that was ninety-nine percent nerves and one percent desperation, she managed to land it in the weedy grass beside the road.

Okay. All right. Mallory's breath came fast and shallow as the kid stalked towards her to snatch up the purse. He was closer now. Almost within reach.

She sucked in her gut, trying to work up the courage to propel her body through the air while he tore open the purse and viewed its meager contents.

She waited a fraction too long.

"Pah!" Pocketing her one credit card, he threw the purse into the weeds again. "There is more, yes?"

"No! Nothing! I swear."

"You come from the château. You are the guest of Madame d'Marchand. You have the suitcase. The furs. The jewels."

"I'm staying at the château, but I don't have any jewels or furs. You've got the wrong girl."

"I think not. Move away."

She took one step to the side. One slightly forward. Another…

Gilbért's groan was hardly more than a whimper, but the small animal sound provided the only distraction Mallory knew she would get. When the kid threw a swift glance over his shoulder, she sprang.

She knocked into his shoulder, threw him off balance, lunged again. This time she hit him from behind.

Locking one arm around his neck, she clung to his back like a monkey and made a desperate grab with her free hand. She caught only a corner of his jacket sleeve, but it was enough to keep him from angling his gun in her direction.

Cursing, he bucked and humped like an enraged bull. Mallory bounced on his back like a rag doll, but wouldn't loosen her stranglehold or release his sleeve. Knowing she had to bring him to his knees before he shook her off, she tightened her arm around his throat and squeezed for all she was worth.

"Mademoiselle!"

From the corner of one eye, she saw Gilbért stagger to his feet.

"He's got a gun!" she shouted.

The possibility Gilbért might join the fray spurred the kid to renewed fury. Choking, he spun in a circle and pumped off wild shots.

The first went into the air. The second plowed into the Rolls' shiny chrome grill. Cordite stung Mallory's eyes. Percussive shock waves hammered at her eardrums, so loud and painful she almost missed the roar of a car tearing down the road at top speed.

The kid picked up on it the same moment she did. Every bit as desperate as Mallory now, he staggered toward the Rolls and spun her into its side. Her hip slammed into the tank-like fender. Pain screamed up her spine.

Still she hung on. Or tried to. A second ramming jarred every bone in her body. Her chokehold loosened. His sleeve tore free of her grasp, but it took a vicious elbow to her ribs to knock her off the bastard's back.

She fell to the pavement. Heard Gilbért shout something in French. Then another shot cracked through the air.

"No!"

Mallory rolled onto all fours, prepared to see the butler stretched out on the pavement, fully expecting she would be next. Instead she heard an unbroken stream of curses from Gilbért, punctuated by the thud of running feet. Her head whipped toward the sound.

Cutter raced toward her from the car skidded sideways across the road some yards back. Mallory's dazed mind registered the pistol gripped in his hand. Gulping, she cranked her head around and spotted the baker's son sprawled face-down in a slowly spreading pool of blood. Her joints turning to jelly, she plopped down.

"Are you hurt?" Cutter crouched beside her, his grim glance raking her from head to toe. "Mallory! Sweetheart! Were you hit?"

"No." She raised a shaking hand to shove back her tangled hair and winced. "Not by a bullet, anyway. Bastard got me with an elbow."

"An elbow?"

"Right in the ribs."

Cutter sat back on his heels. His blood still thundered in his ears. His lungs hadn't pulled in a breath since he'd spotted the humpback figure gyrating wildly beside the Rolls. He'd aged a good ten years when he'd identified Mallory as the hump. Another ten in the two or three seconds it had taken him to jam on the brakes, leap out of the car and yank his Glock from its ankle holster.

"Stay here," he bit out.

Glock in hand, he joined Gilbért. The majordomo was on one knee beside the shooter, feeling for a pulse. Cutter didn't expect him to find one. He hadn't had time for a precision take-down.

"He's dead," Gilbért confirmed.

With a grunt of pain, the older man pushed to his feet. Cutter hooked his arm to help him up.

"You okay?"

"Yes." Disgust riddled his voice. "Like the fool, I turn my back and he hits me from behind."

Cutter kept a steadying hand on Gilbért's arm. His face was ashen and his cap had slipped down over one ear, but otherwise he appeared whole.

"Madame Picard and I feared it would come, sooner or late, with that one."

"You know him?"

"He is Remy Duchette, the son of the baker in town. He's had trouble with the police, you understand, but nothing that makes me think he carries a gun. I would not have stopped if I thought him dangerous."

"Why *did* you stop?"

"Remy comes out of the woods just there and waves to us. I think he wants a ride. Too late it becomes clear he waits for us."

Cutter slewed toward the treeline. The kid had picked a good spot for an ambush. A bend in the road, where the Rolls had to slow to make the turn. Plenty of cover to hide behind until his prey appeared.

"Remy knows this car," Gilbért continued, his disgust mounting with every word. "He knows madame entertains guests of great wealth. He has probably heard in the village that you and mademoiselle stay at the château and decides to wait in hope of robbing you."

"So that's what you think this was? An attempted robbery?"

"*Oui.* I hear him tell mademoiselle he wants her purse and the furs and jewels from her suitcase."

Cutter said nothing, but the warning lights already blipping inside his head flashed a sharper red.

"He said he wanted her suitcase?"

"He wants what is in it. Mademoiselle tells him she has only her purse with her, but he does not believe her and orders her to move away from the car."

"He acted all jumpy and twitchy," Mallory chimed in as she joined them. She gave the sprawled body a quick glance and looked away. "I think he was on drugs. My guess is he needed money for a hit."

"We must call the gendarmes." His face grim,

Gilbért extracted a cell phone from his pocket. "Then I must go into town to explain to my friend the baker how his son dies."

Cutter nodded. The sooner they got the police on the scene, the sooner he could get Mallory back within the walls of the château.

"I'll cover the body. Is there a blanket or a tarp in the car?"

"A tarp, in the trunk."

With the ease of long practice, Cutter reached down, hiked his pants' leg, and slid the Glock into its ankle holster. Mallory followed the movement with a crease between her brows.

Cutter knew he'd blown what little remained of his cover. Before he explained the Glock, though, Ms. Dawes needed to do a little explaining of her own.

"You're still green around the gills." With a firm hand on her elbow, he steered her back to the Rolls. "You'd better sit. It'll take a while for the police to get here."

She eased onto the seat with an awkward movement that told him her ribs were still hurting and sat sideways, shoulders hunched, while he searched the Rolls' cavernous trunk. It yielded both a neatly folded tarp and a supply of emergency road beacons. Cutter set several as a warning to any approaching vehicles to slow down.

He itched to search the woods for evidence that

would either support or disprove Mallory's theory that this was a drug heist gone bad, but he could wait for the police on that. Right now he was more interested in her reasons for departing the château so abruptly.

Hooking an elbow on the open back door, he conducted a swift assessment. Her face had lost its pasty hue, but the crease was still there, pulling at her brows. Cutter knew the questions were piling up behind her frown and decided to slip his in first.

"Madame Picard said you got a phone call and asked Gilbért to take you to the train station. Why didn't you wait for me, tell me where you were going?"

"You were out jogging. I was in a hurry." Her glance dropped to his ankle. "Do you always carry a gun?"

"Most of the time."

"You weren't wearing it last night."

"It wasn't necessary inside the château." Doggedly, he steered the conversation back to her abrupt departure. "Why did you just up and leave this morning, Mallory? Where were you going?"

"I told you. Into town."

"Why?"

"The stationmaster called. He said a package had come for me on the overnight express train from Paris, and that I had to sign for it personally. I thought it had to be either my passport or replacement traveler's checks, so I asked Gilbért to drive me to town."

If Cutter had any doubts about this roadside attack, she'd just resolved them.

Neat, he thought grimly. Very neat. Dangle the bait. Lure the prey out of her protected lair. Arrange an ambush on a deserted stretch of road. The only question in his mind was how the hell the hunter could be sure she would bring her suitcase with her.

"Your turn," Mallory snapped, breaking into his thoughts. "Why do you have a gun strapped to your ankle? Is the wine business so dangerous and cut-throat? Or was that all a lie, too?"

"Pretty much."

Her breath left on a long, slow hiss. "You're starting to really torque me off, Smith."

"Brace yourself, Dawes. It gets worse. I work for the U.S. government. An obscure agency you've never heard of. We've had you under close surveillance since Dulles."

Chapter 11

Mallory sat in the passenger seat of the Rolls. Stunned by Cutter's revelations, she nursed her aching ribs with slow, dazed strokes while he and Gilbért briefed the officer who'd arrived on the scene.

He'd followed her from the Paris airport.

He'd orchestrated every move, from their initial meeting to the passport delays to this romantic getaway at a French château.

He and this shadowy agency he worked for suspected her of stealing personal data on millions of government employees!

Every word, every touch had been a lie.

Last night he'd asked her to trust him, to give him time to make some calls before he filled in the blanks. Fool that she was, she'd tried to talk herself into doing just that.

"Mademoiselle Dawes?"

The police officer's sympathetic face loomed in the window of the Rolls. She and the French gendarmerie were becoming well acquainted, Mallory thought on a bubble of quickly suppressed hysteria.

"I understand this has been a shock, but I must ask you some questions."

The police officer seemed to ascribe her disjointed answers to nerves and the language barrier. Using great patience, he took her statement before speaking once again with Gilbért and Cutter.

Their colloquy resulted in more phone calls and a search of the woods. In the ensuing wait, Mallory's shock gave way to a slow burn as more and more personnel arrived on the scene. The local mortician, who evidently doubled as coroner's assistant, drove up in his hearse. A Crime Scene Unit appeared shortly after that, followed some time later by two men in civilian clothes.

They conducted a lengthy dialogue with Cutter and cast several pointed looks in Mallory's direction but didn't speak to her directly. Accepting the business cards they gave him, Cutter passed them one of his own before striding back to the Rolls.

"Let's go. We'll take my car."

When he reached down to help her, Mallory sent him a look that froze his hand in midair. The message was lethally clear. Touch her and he died.

Ice on the outside, smoldering at her core, she didn't say a word during the short drive. Neither did Cutter. They both knew the thin veneer of silence would shatter once they reached the château. Too many furious questions, too many outraged emotions roiled around inside the confines of the car to keep them bottled up for long.

First, however, they had to get through Madame Picard's barrage of shocked exclamations. Her husband had called and related the gist of the attack, but she needed the assurances of both Mallory and Cutter that Gilbért had sustained no injuries other than a slight dent to his head. After much hand-wringing and head-shaking, the apple-cheeked cook retreated to her domain with promises to deliver a pot of coffee and fresh pastries to the library.

Her footsteps were still ringing on the parquet floor when Cutter braced his hips against the gilt-trimmed desk that dominated the library and eyed Mallory's angry expression.

"You've had time to digest what I told you. I can see it didn't go down well."

"How very astute of you, Mr. Smith. If that's your real name," she added on a scathing note.

"It is. Where do you want to start?"

Arms folded, she faced him across the width of the oriental carpet. "How about this disk you say was in my suitcase."

He nodded, his stance as relaxed as hers was rigid. A framed portrait by an artist Mallory didn't recognize hung in a lighted alcove behind him. All sharp angles and glaring colors, the painting was probably a masterpiece, but she was in no mood to appreciate art right now.

"The disk is a standard, seventy-megabyte CD," Cutter said crisply, "the kind available to every government employee. A baggage inspector at Dulles found it in a side pocket of your suitcase, tucked inside a case for a CD by blues singer Corinne Bailey Rae."

His steady gaze never left her face. Hers lanced into him like a pointed stake aimed at his heart.

"Go on."

"The baggage inspector recognized the General Services Administration logo on the disk and showed it to his supervisor, who popped it into a computer. It contained only one file. I told you what was in it."

"Yes," she ground out, "you did."

She was still struggling with that. After a VA employee admitted he'd loaded millions of personnel files onto a home computer that was stolen in a burglary a few years back, every federal agency had tightened controls over personnel data. Yet someone had used *her* pass code to access *her* computer and collect the names, social security numbers, and financial information on twenty million of her fellow government employees.

"What I didn't tell you," Cutter continued evenly, "was that our lab techs found only your prints on the disk."

If she'd opened a new box of CDs and handled the contents before walking out of Congressman Kent's offices for the last time, Mallory didn't remember it.

"All that proves," she countered, "is the person who put it in my suitcase was very careful."

"Agreed. What we need to do now is determine who that person was."

She supposed she should be grateful for the *we* and for his calm deliberation. Then again, why the hell shouldn't he be calm? She was the one tagged with identity theft on a massive scale.

The possibility she might land in the middle of another media blitz, this time as a suspected traitor, was so demoralizing Mallory had to bite down on the soft inner tissue of her lip to hold back an anguished groan.

The pain helped, but her voice still came out thick and heavy. "I'm not sure I should talk to you about any of this until I consult with a lawyer."

"That's your call, Mallory. We'll work it any way you want."

There it was again, that seductive, sympathetic *we.* As if they were on the same team. Partners. Friends. Lovers.

"But we *have* to work it," he insisted with maddening deliberation. "I don't have any proof at this point, but I suspect this morning's attempted robbery was an attempt to retrieve the disk."

Mallory had pretty much come to the same conclusion. Nothing else made sense, as Cutter proceeded to point out.

"Duchette wasn't there by chance. Someone alerted him to the possibility that you would drive into town this morning to pick up the package waiting for you at the station and, presumably, resume your interrupted vacation. Someone who doesn't know your suitcase floated away with your rental car and is currently resting at the bottom of the Bay of St. Malo."

"The same someone you hoped I would lead you to."

"That's right."

The blunt, unapologetic response ripped a hole in Mallory's heart. She'd convinced herself Cutter was different. Worse, she'd fallen a little bit in love with him. Maybe more than a little.

Even after last night, after he'd dropped that bomb about the dossier, she'd granted him the grace period he'd asked for. Still hoping, still clinging to the ridiculous notion that he hadn't played her for a complete fool, she'd decided to hang around for the explanation he'd promised.

Well, now she had it. She was the bait he wanted to dangle in front of a shadowy, international thug. Hugging her arms to hold in the hurt, Mallory lifted her chin and waited for him to continue.

"We know him only as the Russian. We believe he's responsible for previous coordinated identity thefts, but nothing on quite this scale."

Cutter watched her face and knew he slashed into her with every word. Shoving his hands in his pants' pockets, he balled his fists and carved the next slice.

"We want him, Mallory. *I* want him. He and his kind have caused untold misery to hundreds of thousands of people. This gig would have been bigger, caused even more damage. If he'd gotten his hands on that data, the bastard could have brought our government to a temporary standstill."

"This is all so unreal. And so ironic. Congressman Kent took the floor of the House just a few months ago and gave a speech stressing the urgent need for additional safeguards on personal financial data." Her lips twisted in a mocking smile. "I wrote most of it."

"Which makes you the perfect sacrificial goat if anything went wrong. You possessed an insider's knowledge of the weak links in data protection. You could access restricted systems in your official capacity. You had damned good reason to want to get even with Kent."

"And if I got caught," she said bitterly, "I proved Kent's point. Our information systems are so vulnerable that any disgruntled employee can walk away from the job with a disk full of unauthorized data."

Cutter stiffened. "What did you just say?"

"You heard me. Our systems are so vulner…"

"No! Before that."

"Do you mean the bit about proving the pompous ass's point? Trust me, Kent could turn even a theft by one of his own employees into a political advantage. Not only do I show myself for the predatory female that he painted me, I help get him reelected by making more headlines for him."

"Kent's up for reelection this year?"

"Don't you read the papers?"

"I told you, I've been out of the country." Dismissing her sarcasm with an impatient shake of his head, he strode across the room. "What's the story with Kent? Does he have locks on his seat?"

Startled by his bulldog, in-her-face aggressiveness, Mallory shed some of her own prickly attitude.

"Not this time. He's facing a tough challenge from his state's former lieutenant governor. Or was," she amended, "until the sexual harassment charges I filed edged his competitor out of the headlines and into obscurity. You wouldn't believe how many points Kent gained in the polls after the charges were dismissed. My boss played the noble legislator, wrongly accused, to the hilt."

"Jesus!"

Cutter paced the length of the library and back again, his mind churning with new and intensely disturbing possibilities.

What if they'd followed the wrong scent? What if the Russian wasn't involved? Or involved only on the periphery? What if this was all an elaborate setup, with Mallory fingered to take the fall while racking up more points in the polls for her former boss?

Whirling, he strode back to the woman watching him with wary distrust.

"Sit down," he snapped. "We're going to take this from the top. I want to know who knew you were leaving for France, who had access to your computer, and everyone who stands to gain if and when Congressman Ashton Kent is reelected."

Not until hours later, after they'd expanded the list to include everyone who stood to *lose* if Kent *failed* to win reelection, did they begin to zero in on a name.

By then Gilbért had returned from town and Madame Picard had substituted the tray of untouched pastries with a heaping platter of ham-and-goat-cheese sandwiches. Cutter downed two, but Mallory only picked at the accompanying salad garnished with walnuts and crisp apple slices. She wasn't quite sure what to make of the intense grilling. Was she still a suspect or what?

"This guy, Dillon Porter," Cutter fired at her between man-sized bites. "You say he tried to talk you out of bringing charges against Kent?"

"Dillon is Kent's senior staffer. He's been around the Hill a long time. He knew how tough it would be for me to make the charges stick. He also warned me to expect a vicious media backlash. He hit the bull's-eye on both."

"Is he on Kent's payroll, or a permanent employee of the House Banking and Trade Committee?"

"He works directly for Kent, but…"

"And he's the person you called yesterday to help expedite your passport?"

"Yes, but…"

"What did you tell him? Exactly."

"I didn't speak with him personally, just left a message on his voice mail. I told him I'd lost my passport and had run into a bureaucratic wall trying to get a replacement. I asked him if he could look into it from his end and pull some strings."

"You didn't mention losing anything else?"

"No."

"Nothing about the traveler's checks or rental car or suitcase?"

"No. But I did give him the number here, so he could contact me if necessary."

"Someone with Porter's connections wouldn't have any trouble tracing the number to Madame d'Marchand's country estate."

Cutter downed the last of his sandwich, his jaw working on the crusty bread while afternoon sun poured in through the library windows. Light sparkled on the old, uneven glass and picked out reddish highlights in his dark hair that Mallory had never noticed before.

She wouldn't have noticed them *now* if not for the fact that he'd planted himself in the upholstered armchair set at right angles to hers, with only a round, leather-topped drum table between them. Dusting his hands on a napkin embroidered with the château's crest, he leaned forward and pinned her with a hard look.

"Did this Porter character know you were leaving for France?"

"*Everyone* at the office knew. I'd been saving and planning for it for ages. I—I almost cancelled. The arbitrator took so long to make his determination. But after the decision, I had to get away."

"Did you take your suitcase to the office at any time before you left for Dulles Airport?"

She shook her head.

"You didn't use it when you cleaned out your

desk? Or swing by to say goodbye to friends on your way to the airport?"

"I didn't have many friends left after the hearing." She covered the still-sharp sting of abandonment with a shrug. "Most of the other staffers didn't want their names associated with mine."

In fact, they'd bailed like rats fleeing a burning tenement building. All except Dillon. He'd never once compromised his loyalty to Congressman Kent, yet had offered Mallory brutally honest advice when asked and a shoulder to cry on when she'd chosen not to follow it.

He'd also, she recalled with a sudden catch to her breath, delivered the written copy of the arbitrator's decision.

"What?" Cutter asked, his gaze sharp on her face.

"I just remembered. Dillon stopped by my apartment the day before I left. Just for a few moments, to drop off some paperwork."

"Where was your suitcase?"

"I don't know." She scrubbed the heel of her hand across her forehead, struggling to recall those last, chaotic hours before she'd made her escape. "In the hall closet, I think. Or I may have carried it to the bedroom to start packing."

Cutter didn't need to hear more. Shoving out of his chair, he unclipped his cell phone and stalked to the window. Feet braced, eyes narrowed on the topiaries trimmed into fanciful shapes in the formal garden outside, he waited for Mike Callahan to acknowledge his signal.

He'd already apprised Hawkeye of the incident in the woods. His controller was working the Remy Duchette connection hard, searching for ties to the Russian. Cutter's terse call propelled him in a new and potentially explosive direction.

"Congressman Kent's senior aide?"

Looking as happy as a lion with a thorn embedded in its paw, Lightning shoved a hand through his sun-streaked mane and paced the length of his office.

"Is Slash sure about this?"

"He sounded sure to me," Mike confirmed grimly.

He'd spent most of the afternoon digging into Dillon Porter's past, present and anticipated future. In a town where who you knew carried considerably more weight than what you knew, Porter had racked up an impressive set of credentials. Seventeen years on Capitol Hill, first as a page, then an intern, then a professional staffer, had solidified his power base and made him indispensable to Congressman Kent. The fact that he'd stuck with Kent despite the legislator's rumored extracurricular activities suggested Porter was every bit as ambitious as his boss. Longevity carried its own cachet on the Hill.

"As far as I can tell," Mike informed his boss,

"Porter's clean. I've screened his financials, his contacts with registered lobbyists, every overseas junket he took with his boss. I couldn't find anything that even suggested a link to the Russian."

"So Slash thinks the data theft may be a setup, with the ultimate goal of making Kent look good for pushing for tighter controls over personal financial data?"

"He thinks it's a possibility. Kent was facing a tough challenge for reelection until the publicity resulting from the Dawes allegations painted him as a combination of unjustly accused and sly old dog."

"Knowing Kent, he parlayed both roles into a solid block of votes."

"Yeah, he did. The latest polls indicate the good ol' boys back home are solidly in his camp, but some women voters are still on the fence."

"They'd topple off quick enough if Mallory Dawes was branded a thief as well as an oversexed temptress."

"That's the working hypothesis."

Lightning shoved back his suit coat and splayed his hands on his hips. He knew as well as Mike they were walking a political minefield here. The President himself had stumped for his good pal and longtime political crony. Kent's reelection was essential to the party's midterm legislative agenda.

"What's your game plan, Hawk?"

"I'm going to get up close and personal with Porter. He doesn't know me from squat but, seasoned staffer that he is, he'll certainly know that the Military Marksmanship Association has more than ten thousand members."

Not to mention strong ties to the NRA. Mike had his opinions about gun control, which didn't necessarily coincide with those held by many of his fellow sharpshooters. He suspected Dillon Porter would see only dollar signs, however, when he linked Mike with the powerful lobbying organization.

"When are you going to establish contact?"

"Tonight. I obtained a copy of Porter's schedule. He's on the Hill until six, then he and his boss head over to a reception in honor of the new Secretary General of the World Bank."

"The World Bank?" A smile spread across Lightning's tanned face. "Well, well."

Mike matched Nick's grin. They couldn't have orchestrated the initial contact any better if they'd planned it. Adam Ridgeway, OMEGA's former director, now headed the International Monetary Fund, the operating arm of the World Bank.

Keying his intercom, Lightning summoned his executive assistant into the office.

"Do you know what your folks have on the agenda tonight, Jilly?"

"They're attending a function for the IMF. Wayland and I were supposed to go with them but he had to fly up to New York on a case. Why? What's the deal?"

"Hawk wants to connect with someone attending the soiree."

Her glance slid to Mike. He'd steeled himself for the impact of those sapphire eyes…or thought he had. Damned if it didn't hit him with the force of a 40mm rubber-tipped, riot-control bullet.

"That works out perfectly. You can be my escort."

The protest came fast and straight from his gut. "That's not a good idea."

"Sure it is. I'll be your cover, Hawk. Pick me up at seven."

Chapter 12

Mike had landed in a number of desperate situations since joining OMEGA. He couldn't ever remember feeling as hinky as he did when he pulled into the circular drive leading to the home of Gillian Ridgeway's parents, however.

Set on a wooded lot in McLean's priciest neighborhood, the two-story brick residence wore a graceful patina of age. Ivy climbed up the mellow brick. Boxwoods framed the walk to the door. Leafy maples and oaks shaded the house, molting bright layers of orange and red onto the carpet of lawn.

Mike drove up the circular drive and parked his

newly washed Blazer under the pillared portico. The scent of wood smoke filled his lungs as he mounted the front steps. One thought filled his head.

This was an assignment. Just an assignment. Gillian Ridgeway's sole purpose was to provide an entrée into her father's set. With that admonition firmly in mind, Mike rolled his shoulders to settle his tux and leaned on the doorbell.

Instant chaos erupted inside. When the door jerked open a moment later, the noise shot up another ten or twenty decibels. Maggie and Adam's teenaged son added to it by bellowing at the top of his lungs.

"Would you please *shut up!*"

The sheepdog lunging frantically in the kid's hold ignored the booming command. Tongue lolling, jowls flapping, it howled an ecstatic welcome and went up on its back legs to paw the air. Mike was treated to a hairy chest, a freckled pink belly, and a sack of balls that would have made a stallion strut. The dog was hung like a Clydesdale.

"Shut up, I said!"

Grunting with the effort, Adam Ridgeway II— Tank to everyone who knew him—hauled on the hound's collar to drag him away from the door. Dark-haired and brown-eyed like his mother, the kid gave every indication he'd soon match or exceed his father's height. Both parents lived in mortal fear of the not-very-distant day Tank would qualify for his learner's permit and hit the streets.

"Sorry 'bout that," he shouted over the still-ecstatic barking. "He's just a pup. Hasn't learned to mind real well yet."

No kidding.

"C'mon in." Planting his sneakered feet, Tank struggled to control the leaping, cavorting animal. "Been meaning to ask you. When are we going to the range?"

Thankfully, Maggie's intervention saved Mike from having to answer. Grimacing at the unceasing din, she shouted over the rail of the circular stairs.

"Tank, please! Take him outside."

Muscles straining under his maroon-and-gold Washington Redskins sweatshirt, the teen hauled the hound down the hall.

The sheepdog thought the rough handling was great fun. His claws scrabbled on the marble tiles. His tail scissored back and forth. He made repeated lunges, woofing joyously and almost knocking Tank on his butt several times before both disappeared through a side door.

"Sorry, Mike." Smiling ruefully, Maggie Sinclair, code name Chameleon, descended the rest of the stairs. "Radizwell Senior passed all of his energy and none of his manners to his numerous offspring."

The original Radizwell had exhibited even less re-

straint than his progeny, but Mike knew better than
to badmouth Maggie's beloved pet. The Hungarian
sheepdog, along with a completely obnoxious lizard
she'd picked up during a mission to Central America,
had ruled the Ridgeway household for as long as
anyone could remember.

Radizwell I had succumbed to old age after
spawning several successive generations. Terence
the Lizard was still around. Somewhere. Mike snuck
a quick look at the chandelier gracing the entryway
to make sure the evil-tempered creature wouldn't
drop down on his head before taking the hands
Maggie held out to him.

"I believe this is the first time I've seen you in a
tux, Hawkeye. You look very distinguished."

"You look pretty darn good yourself, Chameleon."

She looked better than good. Her slinky black
cocktail dress hugged a figure that could still turn
heads on any street in any city. Laugh lines fanned
the skin at the corners of her sparkling brown eyes,
but those tiny wrinkles were the only indication she
could have a daughter Gillian's age, another in
college, and a son as tall and skinny as a scarecrow.

"Jilly's almost ready. While we wait, you can brief
Adam and me on what's going down."

Tucking her arm in his, she steered Mike into the
den. Her husband was already there. As cool and
contained as Maggie was warm and spontaneous,

Adam Ridgeway looked up from the pitcher of martinis he was stirring. The gleam that lit his eyes when they skimmed over his wife was nine parts admiration, one part smug male possession.

"New dress?"

"Yes, it is. Do you like it?"

"Very much. Hello, Hawk. Martini?"

"I'll pass, thanks."

Nodding, Ridgeway passed his wife a long-stemmed glass. His gaze turned several degrees cooler when he took his own glass in hand.

"Have a seat," he invited in a tone that had Mike unconsciously squaring his shoulders, "and tell me just what kind of op you've involved my daughter in."

Mike thought the grilling by the father was bad. Making the rounds at the crowded reception with the daughter's body tucked against him was worse.

Much worse.

Gillian had dressed for the occasion in a strapless, flame silk sheath that revealed more than it concealed. Decorated with tiny beads that sparkled when they caught the light, the dress and its wearer drew every eye in the place, including Mike's.

She'd added killer three-inch stilettos in the same heart-stopping red that brought her shoulder almost level with his. She'd also swept her thick black hair up in a cluster of curls that left her neck bare except for the tiny baby hairs on her nape. Those soft, feathery curls snagged his eye every time she turned to greet another friend or acquaintance. Since she seemed to know everyone in the place, every curl had burned into Mike's brain by the time he spotted Congressman Kent.

His face animated beneath his carefully styled silver mane, the legislator was evidently relating some inside joke to a circle of cronies. When he finished, the men around him burst into raucous laughter. The lone woman in the group rolled her eyes.

Mike's nerves began to hum with something other than acute awareness of the woman on his arm. Wherever Kent was, his aide wouldn't be far away.

A moment later, Gillian leaned closer. "There's Porter," she murmured. "Second in line at the bar. Gray suit, yellow striped tie, rimless glasses."

The staffer looked a good five years older than the photo in the file Mike had pulled up. Then again, bag-carrying someone like Kent would probably add years to anyone. He was still on the job, Mike saw, working the line at the bar, engaging both the man ahead and the one behind with the skill essential to a politician's aide.

Mike bided his time until Porter had procured two drinks and delivered one to his boss. Kent took it with a careless nod and turned back to his cronies. His aide lingered at the edge of the group for a few moments before drifting toward a newscaster for one of the local affiliates.

"Okay, Jilly. Let's move in."

Cutter received Mike's update early the next morning, European time.

He was just out of the shower after a grueling dawn run. He'd needed the run to clear the cobwebs from his head. If he'd slept more than a few hours last night, he'd be surprised. His mind had gnawed restlessly at the problem of the stolen data. The rest of him had remained tense and edgy, all too aware of the fact that Mallory slept just on the other side of the connecting door.

Only two nights ago she'd flamed in his arms. He could still feel her body taut and straining under his, still hear her hoarse groan when she'd climaxed. He'd come within an ace of knocking on that door a half dozen times and trying his damndest to recover the ground he'd lost with her.

He might have done it if she hadn't been wrung dry by the incident in the woods yesterday morning, not to mention the grilling he'd put her through for most of the afternoon. After that exhausting session, she'd opted for a tray in her room and an evening on her own to try and sort through everything he'd dumped on her.

The report Cutter had just received from Mike

wasn't going to help with the sorting. Slicking back hair still damp from his shower, he rapped on the connecting door.

Mallory took her time answering. The dark smudges under her eyes suggested she hadn't slept any better than he had. Bundled from neck to ankle in a plush terrycloth robe, she read the news on his face.

"Your friends didn't find anything on Dillon, did they?"

"Not yet. They're still digging, but at this point he looks squeaky clean."

Too clean, in Mike and Cutter's collective judgment. Everyone had skeletons in their closet. Porter couldn't have spent all those years at the center of power without acquiring one or two himself.

"So we're back to square one," Mallory muttered wearily. "With me dangling at the end of your hook, bait for this Russian character."

"Let's talk about that."

When she sank onto the edge of the rumpled bed, her robe parted at the knee. Not much. Only enough to give Cutter a glimpse of smooth, bare calf. Ruthlessly, he slammed the lid on the insidious thought that Ms. Dawes was halfway to naked. He'd done some hard thinking in the dark hours before dawn.

"I think it's time to switch gears. That incident yesterday morning scared the crap out of me." Cutter wasn't going to forget seeing her go down any time soon. "I don't want you hurt, Mallory."

The admission elicited a small huff. "I'm not real thrilled at the prospect, either."

"If Remy Duchette's attack *was* linked to an attempt to retrieve the disk, whoever wants the data is getting both frustrated and desperate. That makes him dangerous. We need to send him a signal, make it clear you don't have the CD."

"How do you plan to accomplish that?"

"We'll use the media."

"Please tell me you're kidding!"

"I know, I know. They ate you alive at home. With a few words dropped in the right ears, they'll do the same here."

Cutter hated the idea of feeding her to the sharks again but didn't see any other option at this point.

"We'll put you in front of the cameras. Have you relate your sad tale of the riptide carrying off your rental. You'll stress that you lost everything, including your suitcase and all its contents. Then I put you on a plane back to the States and hang around Mont St. Michel to see if someone tries to recover the disk."

Manfully, he kept his gaze on her face while she fiddled with the flap of her robe and mulled over his plan. He could see it didn't thrill her.

"I know you came to France to escape the media, Mallory. I don't like asking you to put yourself out there again, but it's the only way I could think of to throw any would-be predators off your scent."

"I can handle the media."

"What the problem, then?"

Dammit, he wished she'd stop playing with the flap of her robe. The thick fabric bunched, was smoothed flat, bunched again. Cutter was starting to sweat when she finally voiced her objections to his plan.

"I skipped lunch for almost a year to save for this trip. It started as a vacation, but morphed into my escape from the ugliness at home. I'm not ready to wade back into the mess yet."

"I understand. I do."

He'd watched her unfold during those hours in the sun, when they'd sipped Calvados and picnicked with Monsieur Villieu and his wife under the apple trees. Warm color had dusted her cheeks. Laughter had sparkled in her eyes. Now the shadows were back, and it ate at Cutter's insides that he'd been the one to put them there.

"You can't just pick up your vacation where you left off," he said quietly. "Not while whoever put that disk in your suitcase thinks you might still have it."

Chewing on her lower lip, she smoothed the ter-rycloth several more times.

"Okay," she said after a moment, "here's *my* plan. We orchestrate the media blitz as you suggest. I admit

I lost everything. Let the world know my suitcase went to sea with my rental car. Then, after we've thrown whoever wants the disk off my scent, as you so delicately put it, I go my way and you go yours."

"No good."

The swift, uncompromising negative took her aback. "Why not?"

"I can't let you wander around the countryside on your own."

"Let?" she echoed, stiffening.

"I'll rephrase that. I don't want you wandering around France on your own. There's no guarantee this media ploy will work. Word that you don't have the disk in your possession might not reach the right people. Or they may not believe it. You could still be a target, Mallory. I can't… I don't want to take that risk."

"If they think I still have the data, I wouldn't be any safer at home than I am here."

Yes, she would. Cutter had requested 24/7 surveillance for Mallory and her apartment. She wouldn't take a step without someone right there, behind or beside her.

He couldn't tell her about the tag, however. Not yet. *He* was convinced she hadn't stolen the data but until he proved it, she'd remain under watchful eyes.

"We don't have to decide this right now," he said with a shrug that suggested her imminent return to the States wasn't a done deal. "Let me dangle the bait, see if we can gin up some media interest. You may be ready to go home after dealing with them."

"After they start feasting on my flesh again, you mean. You're probably right."

Her shoulders slumped under the robe. He could almost hear her desperate hopes for obscurity crash down around her.

"Okay," she conceded after a long silence, "we'll play it your way."

Knowing that his mission took precedence over her vacation plans didn't stop Cutter from feeling like a total heel.

"You'll have other opportunities to wander through the countryside, Mallory. I promise."

Her chin lifted. A healthy anger leapt back into her eyes. "I don't want your sympathy, Smith, and I sure as hell don't trust your promises."

She pushed off the bed, dismissing him with an imperious, impatient flap of her hand.

"Go do whatever you need to do. I'll start pulling on my body armor. Again."

Cutter's strategy worked exactly as planned.

Ordinarily, a botched robbery and the death of a small-time local hood like Remy Duchette wouldn't stir much interest outside the immediate vicinity. The fact that Duchette had attempted to rob a guest of a famous Paris designer upped the interest considerably. All it took was one call from Hawk to make sure the word leaked to the right ears.

The local stations began calling the château soon after lunch. Following the agreed-on game plan, Mallory refused to grant any interviews. She knew all too well there was nothing like a reluctant subject to rouse the media's hunting instincts.

Sure enough, by the time the early-evening news hit the airwaves, reporters had linked Mallory to the woman who'd made so many headlines back in the States. A stringer for Reuters had also connected her to the police report filed by the gendarme at Mont St. Michel. The phone rang incessantly from then on.

Every major network carried the story on the late-night news. Writhing inside, Mallory huddled in a corner of the sofa in the downstairs sitting room and watched replays of her exit from the Rayburn Congressional Office Building after the arbitrator's ruling that there was insufficient evidence to support her allegation of sexual harassment. Sunglasses shielded her eyes, but her rigid shoulders and tight jaw telegraphed her disgust at the decision. The networks followed her terse replies of "No comment" with excerpts of a news conference held by a smug, vindicated Ashton Kent.

"Bastard," Cutter muttered as the phone shrilled yet again.

As instructed, Gilbért took names and numbers and advised that Mademoiselle Dawes would return the call should she decide to speak about her recent unfortunate experiences. When he delivered the message to the sitting room, Cutter hit the remote to mute the TV.

"We've stirred the pot enough. Please call them back and tell them Ms. Dawes will speak to the press tomorrow at eleven."

"Yes, of course."

"We'll leave for Paris shortly after that. Ms. Dawes wishes to return to the States. I'm putting her on a plane tomorrow afternoon."

"Most understandable." The butler's glance shifted to Mallory. "I am so sorry, mademoiselle, that you will take home such unpleasant memories of your visit to Normandy."

"They're not all unpleasant." She dredged up a smile. "I stayed in this beautiful château, had my first taste of Calvados and sampled Madame Picard's *veau de la Normandie*. Those memories I'll cherish."

There were others, ones she wasn't so sure about. Like the memory of Gilbért crumpling to the ground and skinny, spike-haired Remy Duchette pointing his pistol at her middle. And Cutter…

She didn't look at him. She couldn't. She knew darn well her memories of him would remain as confused as the emotions he roused in her. Worse, she suspected the remembered feel of his mouth and hands and sleek, powerful body surging into hers would blot out her anger at his lies and deception. Eventually.

But she wasn't there yet. She wasn't anywhere near there.

"You must come again," Gilbért pleaded. "Perhaps in the spring, when the apple and pear trees bloom. They shed their petals and cover the earth like snow."

"Perhaps I will."

When he departed the sitting room, Mallory decided to do the same.

"I'm going upstairs. It's been a long day."

Long and draining and filled with mounting dread over the ordeal she'd face tomorrow. She refused to link that hollow feeling in the pit of her stomach to the fact that she'd say goodbye to Cutter shortly after the news conference.

He'd lied to her since day one, for pity's sake! She should be overjoyed to put an ocean between them.

"I'll see you in the morning."

Cutter nodded. Much as he ached to take her in his arms and kiss away her weariness, it was better this way. She'd be on her way home tomorrow, out of his reach until he wrapped up this op.

Now if only he could get her out of his head.

He stayed downstairs until well past midnight. No light showed under the connecting door when he let himself into his suite. Wavering between relief and regret, Cutter stripped down to his shorts, slid between the sheets, and locked his hands under his head.

The sea murmured restlessly outside. Inside, the castle settled into sleepy semisilence. The wind whistled down stone chimneys. An occasional water pipe pinged. The clock on the mantel bonged the quarter hour, then the half.

Cutter had resigned himself to another long night when one sound separated itself from the rest. His glance zinged to the connecting door. Not so much as a sliver of light showed under the sill.

He picked up another soft creak. Two seconds later he was out of bed and dragging on his slacks. His head told him that it was probably Gilbért or his wife coming up the stairs with such a stealthy tread, trying not to disturb the guests. His gut said different. Sliding his Glock from its holster, he put his back to the wall and cracked the bedroom door.

A shadow slid over the top step. Elongated. Danced along the darkened hallway.

The shape was stretched and distorted. Cutter could see it belonged to neither Picard. Eyes narrowed, blood pumping, he thumbed the Glock's safety but didn't shove through the door until a loud clatter shattered the silence.

Chapter 13

"Dammit!"

As if tripping over a creaking stair wasn't bad enough, Mallory hit the oak railing on her way down and landed on her butt with a jarring thud.

Her late-night snack flew off the plate she'd carried up with her. The cheese slices she'd cut from the towel-wrapped wheel Madame Picard had left out landed in her lap. The round-bladed knife she'd brought to spread it with scattered with a half dozen or so crackers. A ripe, juicy apple bounced down the stair, ponging noisily on each tread.

Mallory managed to catch the pear before it

suffered a similar fate, then lost her grip on it when a nasty snarl came out of the darkness behind her.

"What the hell are you doing, creeping around at this time of night?"

"Me!" Her heart pinging, she threw an indignant glance over her shoulder at the half-naked male who materialized out of the shadows. "You just took five years off my life…and no doubt bruised my pear!"

"Was that what went airborne?" The taut set to his shoulders relaxed. "Hang loose, I'll retrieve it for you."

First he detoured to the lacquered chest at the top of the stairs and deposited an object that gleamed dully in the faint light. Mallory's pulse bumped when she realized he'd come into the hall armed.

"There's an apple down there somewhere, too."

He descended the stairs like a sleek jungle cat. His bare feet didn't raise so much as a creak on the stairs that had protested *her* weight. The dim light made a moonscape of his back and shoulders and deepened the gap that appeared between his low-riding slacks and the small of his back when he stooped to retrieve the runaway fruit.

"What did you do?" he asked, dropping down to sit knee-to-knee with her on the step. "Raid the fridge?"

"The kitchen table. Madame Picard left a platter of goodies out."

"I'm going to miss that woman." Cutter eyed the recovered stash hopefully. "Got enough for two?"

"If you don't mind broken crackers and slightly dented fruit."

"Feed me, woman."

So much had happened since Mallory boarded the plane to Paris that she would have sworn she was beyond being surprised by anything. Yet here she was, huddled on the stairs of a centuries-old château in a borrowed bathrobe with a man who'd lied to her from their first meeting. What surprised her even more was that she was in no hurry to end their late night tête-à-tête.

Frowning, she tried to rekindle her earlier anger. She was still seriously ticked at Cutter. Not to mention hurt that he'd used her as a pawn in his dangerous game. So why was she spreading cheese flavored with crunchy hickory nuts for him?

Because she was leaving tomorrow, the nasty voice of reality mocked. Leaving France. Leaving Yvette d'Marchand's château. Leaving him. Her dream-vacation-that-never-quite-was would be over. All she had left of it was a few more hours and this temporary, fragile truce with Cutter.

Refusing to dwell on the grim reality of going home to hunt for a job and an employer who'd hire someone who'd made allegations against her previous boss, she spread a cracker with the soft, creamy cheese.

"Here."

Cutter popped the cracker into his mouth. While he crunched down, Mallory cut and peeled a slice of pear with the blunt-tipped knife. The fruit was firm and succulent. Juice dribbled onto her palm with each cut.

She gave Cutter the first bite and nibbled on the second. He munched contentedly, his elbows resting on the stair behind him. Mallory licked the juice from her fingers and let her glance slide along his outstretched length.

Shadows played across his flat belly and sculpted the planes of his chest. The air in the drafty hall was cool enough to make her grateful for the fluffy robe, but Cutter seemed impervious to the chill.

"I've arranged to have someone meet you at the airport in D.C.," he told her, breaking the stillness.

"Why?"

"I thought you might need a friend."

"A friend? Or a watchdog?"

"Both," he admitted without a trace of apology. "His name is Mike Callahan. He'll keep you safe until I wrap things up over here."

She didn't particularly care for the idea that she had to be "kept" by anyone, but the incident in the woods had shaken her more than she was ready to admit.

"What happens when you wrap things up?" she asked. "You resume watchdog duties yourself?"

"If we haven't nailed whoever slipped that disk into your suitcase."

"And if you have?"

"Then I'm hoping you might still want a friend."

She didn't have many of those left, Mallory acknowledged silently. Yet the idea of being Cutter's pal turned the sweet taste of pear sour and left an empty feeling in the pit of her stomach.

She was still trying to deal with the hollow sensation when he levered upright. His shoulder nudging hers, he angled around and removed the knife from her sticky hands.

"Just a precaution," he said when she raised a brow. "The thing is, I'd like to be more than friends. And I really want to kiss you right now."

"We both know that's not a good idea."

"Granted. That doesn't make the want go away."

He cupped her cheek. His palm was warm against her skin, his breath a soft wash that mingled with hers. Mere inches separated them. Tomorrow, it would be an ocean. After that, who knew?

Maybe that was why Mallory didn't pull back when he leaned in, why her head tilted and her lids drifted down. Tomorrow, she decided as his lips brushed hers, would just have to take care of itself.

His mouth moved over hers, tasting, tempting. Heat stirred in her veins. The muscles low in her belly clenched. Then Cutter slid his palm from her cheek to her nape, anchoring her head, and molded his mouth to hers.

The half-eaten pear rolled off Mallory's lap and thumped down the stairs again. The broken crackers scattered. She had no idea where the cheese slices went and didn't care. Her body eager, her hands greedy, she matched him move for move.

Within moments she was semiprone on the wide wooden stairs. His free hand yanked at the tie to her robe. The lapels parted, exposing her to chill air and Cutter's smooth, hot flesh.

She could feel him hard and straining against her hip. Wiggling a little, she added to the pressure on his fly. The sensual friction soon had him grunting and dragging his mouth from hers.

"If we're going to stop," he rasped, "it had better be now."

Her blood pumped in heavy spurts. Desire raced like liquid fire through her veins. She wanted him naked and locked between her thighs.

"If we *don't* stop, we need to change positions. Or geography. This stair tread is putting a permanent dent in my spine."

"That, Ms. Dawes, is easily remedied."

He scooped her up and took the stairs two at a time, reminding Mallory of that powerful scene from *Gone with the Wind*. Except she wasn't Vivien Leigh, fighting him every step of the way and her Clark

Gable retained presence of mind enough to retrieve his gun before striding down the hall toward his half-open bedroom door.

The hard butt of the pistol handle against her hip sobered Mallory and reminded her again why Cutter was here...until he kicked the door shut and carried her to bed in the finest Rhett Butler style.

The scent of fresh-baked croissants pulled Mallory from total unconsciousness. Lifting her face from the satin-covered pillow, she blinked owlishly and followed the general direction of her nose until her sleepy gaze collided with Cutter's.

"'Bout time you woke up."

He, obviously, had been up for some time. His jogging suit lay over the arm of the chair. Muddy sneakers sat on the floor beside it. He must have gotten in an early run, showered and changed while she remained dead to the world.

As he deposited a tray on the bedside table, the tang of his aftershave teased Mallory's nostrils and vied for supremacy with the yeasty scent of the rolls. Wiggling upright, she shoved her hair out of her eyes and helped herself.

"What time is it?" she asked around a flaky mouthful.

"Almost ten."

"Ten!" The croissant lodged partway down her

throat. With a painful gulp, she swallowed the half-chewed bite. "I'm supposed to go in front of the cameras at eleven! Why did you let me sleep?"

"You told me to. Remember?"

Now she did. She'd mumbled the order sometime after her second out-of-body experience. Or was it her third? As best as Mallory could recall, every inch of her had shivered with delight and exhaustion.

Those emotions contrasted starkly with the ones that crept over her now. The prospect of facing a barrage of reporters stripped away all trace of morning-after joy. Her arms as heavy as lead, she dropped the roll back onto the tray.

"I'd better get dressed. Think I could fit into one of those suits of armor in the hall?"

Cutter was well aware of her reluctance to put herself out there again, but her attempt at levity brought home just how deeply she dreaded it. Nudging her aside, he sat on the edge of the mattress.

"I'll be right there with you."

"That's another thing. How do I explain you?" Frowning, she plucked at the bedcovers. "What's our story, Cutter? Do we have a history, or are you just one more notch on my bedpost?"

"If the subject comes up…"

"Trust me," she said bitterly, "it will."

"…we tell them we met in France, fell for each other and aren't worried about the past, only the future."

"They won't buy it." Dragging the covers with her, she slumped against the padded headboard. "We've known each other less than a week. Hardly long enough to fall in love."

For her, maybe. Cutter wasn't sure when he'd taken the plunge.

He suspected it was there in Monsieur Villieu's orchard, with the sunlight on her face and her laughter as potent as the apple brandy. Whenever it had happened, he knew he wanted her safe and this op over more than he'd ever wanted anything. Or anyone.

He'd loved only once before, or thought he had. Jogging along the mist-shrouded cliffs this morning he'd realized that whatever he'd felt for Eva Hendricks didn't come close to the protective and fiercely primitive instincts Mallory Dawes roused in him.

Which was only one of the reasons he'd made a quick trip into town after his run. The other was the horde that would descend on her in less than an hour.

"Maybe this will convince the reporters we're serious."

He positioned the jeweler's box on the tray beside the basket of croissants. Her brow snapping into a line, she stared at the blue velvet box suspiciously.

"What's that?"

"Your protective armor."

The ring was an antique, its square-cut diamond mounted on a wide, white-gold filigree band that looked like old Victorian lace. Smaller baguettes circled the central stone in a delicate swirl.

"There was only one jeweler in town, so I didn't have much of a selection to choose from."

With Mallory watching in slack-jawed surprise, Cutter slipped the ring out of the box and onto her finger. The band was a little loose. He'd had to guess at the size.

"You didn't have to do this," she said, still frowning.

"Yeah, I did."

Feeling as though the moment required a more extravagant gesture, Cutter raised her hand and dropped a kiss on her fingers.

"If you look at the filigree closely, you'll see it's carved in the shape of vines and fruit. Apropos, wouldn't you say?"

She studied it in silence for several moments before lifting her gaze to his. "It's beautiful, Cutter, and will certainly add credibility to our story. I'll give it back to you right after the press conference."

"The ring is yours, Mallory. A souvenir of your trip to France."

Ignoring her protests, he dropped another kiss on her hand and pushed off the bed.

"You'd better get dressed. A couple of TV crews have already arrived to set up their equipment."

* * *

For long moments after the door closed behind Cutter, Mallory simply sat amid the rumpled covers and stared at the white-gold band.

If she'd searched every store in Paris, she couldn't have found a ring that delighted her more. She loved the antique look to it, with the graceful swirl of baguettes anchoring the center stone. But it was the delicate filigree band that filled her heart with a bittersweet ache.

The intricate vines, the tiny leaves, the fruit—as Cutter said, so very apropos of Normandy and the short time they'd spent here. She couldn't believe he'd gone to so much trouble to erect the facade they'd present to the media, or that he'd found such a perfect vehicle to do it.

Then presented it to her here, she thought on a sigh. Amid the rumpled covers, with her hair a tangled mess and her eyes still gritty from sleep. The man needed to work on his timing, if not his technique. Even a fake engagement warranted brushed hair and teeth. With another sigh, she threw off the covers and padded to the bathroom.

She left the blue bedroom thirty minutes later. Rather than appear in borrowed feathers, she wore the jeans, white blouse, and navy blazer she'd had on when she arrived in France. Luckily, the ever efficient

Madame Picard had restored them to pristine neatness. The ring sparkling on her left hand demanded something better than rubber-soled mocs, however. Making her final appearance in a pair of Yvette d'Marchand's exclusive designs, Mallory descended the grand staircase.

A brief smile settled around her heart as she remembered going *up* the stairs the night before, but it died when she spotted the equipment cases scattered across the black-and-white tiles of the entry hall. A babble of voices rose from the library, punctuated by intermittent flashes as the camera crews tested their strobes.

Dread coiled and writhed like a living thing in Mallory's stomach. Dragging in quick, shallow breaths, she forced herself to continue down the stairs.

"Elle est là!"

She had no trouble translating the excited exclamation. Her throat closing, she heard the others pick up the cry.

"There she is!"

"It's her!

Like baying hounds on the trail of a fox, a dozen or so reporters spilled out of the library into the hall. Mallory froze as still cameras flashed, blinding her with a barrage of white light. The questions flew fast and furious until Cutter's deep voice sliced through the din.

"Ms. Dawes will be more than happy to answer your questions, but not here in the hall."

Tall and authoritative, his scars a deliberate and very visible warning that he wasn't a man to be taken lightly, he mounted the stairs and tucked Mallory's hand in his arm. She managed not to clutch at his sleeve like a frightened child, but her knees felt like the custard filling in one of Madame Picard's pastries as they waded into the fray.

"Ladies. Gentlemen," Cutter said calmly. "In the library, as agreed."

A battery of TV cameras, some mounted on tripods, some shoulder-held, captured their entrance. Cutter positioned Mallory in front of the gilt-trimmed desk and slipped a lover-like arm around her waist. The modernistic portrait in its lighted alcove formed a dramatic backdrop. The oriental carpet provided a tapestry of jeweled colors at their feet.

Mallory tried not to wince as the klieg lights came on, adding their glare to the flashes from the still cameras. Boom mikes poked over the heads of reporters who machine-gunned the questions at her.

"Mademoiselle Dawes, how do you come to be at Yvette d'Marchand's château?"

"Did you know Remy Duchette?"

"What happened at Mont St. Michel that caused you to miss the turn of the tide?"

"Have you been in contact with Congressman Kent during your time in France?"

"Is Monsieur Smith your latest lover?"

Mallory knifed the reporter who'd shouted the last question with an icy glare. Before she could respond, however, Cutter drew her closer within the circle of his arm.

"Not her latest," he corrected.

He smiled at her, playing to the audience yet somehow giving her the sense that his words were for her alone.

"Her last."

Okay, this was only pretend. A very skillful act for the cameras. Even if it hadn't been, Mallory knew better than to believe Cutter's smooth lies. That didn't prevent a raw, scratchy lump the size of the Eiffel Tower from clogging her throat.

Chapter 14

If Cutter hadn't already suspected he was in over his head where Mallory Dawes was concerned, watching her perform for the cameras would have done the trick.

He knew how much she'd dreaded the inquisition. Felt her flinch as the questions went from personal and prying to just plain vicious. Chin high, she responded to those questions she chose to while ignoring the rest.

Cutter deflected as many of the barbs as he could by referring all inquiries about Remy Duchette to the local police. He also played the new man in Mallory's life to the hilt, staking his claim with every possessive smile. Yet not even this very public branding could protect her from increasingly salacious questions about her alleged affair with Congressman Kent. Finally, he'd had enough.

"That's it," he said abruptly, fighting hard to keep his anger in check. "Ms. Dawes and I need to leave for the airport. Gilbért will show you out."

Leaving the gaggle to pack up their gear under the butler's watchful eye, Cutter steered Mallory into the hall. She kept her arm tucked in his and a smile pasted on her face as they mounted the stairs. Once out of camera reach, though, she wilted right before his eyes.

"You okay?"

"Yes." A shudder rippled through her slender frame. "I know they're only doing their job. They just…kind of get to me."

"You didn't let it show."

"You think?" She gave a small laugh. "I must be getting better at this. God knows I've had plenty of practice. When do you want to leave?"

"As soon as you get your things together."

This time the laugh was a little more genuine. "That won't take long."

"Knock on the connecting door when you're ready."

Mallory entered the room she'd come to think of as her own and rested her shoulder blades against the door. The circus downstairs had drained and humiliated her, but she regretted more the fact that her stay in this elegant suite with its shimmering azure drapes and four-poster bed was over. That, and the knowledge she would soon say goodbye to Cutter.

She wanted to believe his promise to follow her home as soon as he could. Ached to believe the hours they'd spent locked in each other's arms last night had seared him as much as they had her. Despite his lies and elaborate deceptions, everything inside her wanted to trust him.

Catching her lower lip between her teeth, she raised her left hand. Cutter had insisted she keep the ring. As a souvenir. Curling her hand into a fist, Mallory tilted it this way and that, setting off colorful sparks as the diamonds caught the light.

Her hand stilled. The rainbow of colors dimmed. Sighing, she went to gather her few things.

"You must come again," Gilbért pronounced on the steps leading to the cobbled courtyard. His wife endorsed that with a vigorous bob of her head.

"I cook for you," she promised. "Pears *en croute,* yes? With buttered brandy sauce."

That alone was enough to make Mallory wish she had more to give them as a parting gift than the bottle of Calvados from Monsieur Villieu's private stock.

They, in turn, presented a hibiscus-colored shopping bag with gold cord handles and an instantly recognizable logo. A shoebox sat inside the bag.

"These are from madame's spring collection," Gilbért said. "She hopes you will accept them with her apologies that you should come to harm while a guest in her home."

Lust and guilt battled for Mallory's soul. "I can't accept such an expensive gift."

"But you must," the butler insisted, pressing the bag into her hands. "Madame wishes you to have them."

She suspected it was Gilbért and his wife who wanted her to return home with something other than a mixed bag of memories and the bruises she'd collected from Remy.

"Thank you." Going up on tiptoe, she kissed his weathered cheeks. "And you, Madame Picard."

"*Au revoir,* mademoiselle, *et bonne chance.*"

Cutter stowed his carryall and the small tote holding the items Mallory had purchased in town in the backseat of his rental car. After shaking hands with Gilbért and dropping kisses on Madame Picard's apple-red cheeks, he settled Mallory in the passenger seat and slid behind the wheel. She twisted around to wave as the car rattled through the arched passageway. Once they were on the sweeping drive, the château dwindled to a fanciful, turreted image in the side mirror.

Mallory said little during the long drive to the airport on the outskirts of Paris. Cutter, by contrast, was a whirlwind of activity. Dividing his attention between the traffic ahead and the road behind, he eliminated every obstacle Mallory had been tripping over for the past week. By the time they nosed into the bumper-to-bumper traffic on the airport loop, he had everything arranged.

"Your temporary passport was delivered to the Delta Business Class reservations desk. It's waiting for you with your ticket."

"Okay."

"There's an American Express kiosk inside the terminal. They'll reissue your traveler's checks."

Horns blared as he cut the wheel and pulled onto the ramp for short-term parking.

"The rental-car company wants you to sign a release of liability, but you can take care of that when you get home. Mike Callahan will be at the gate when you deplane. Look for a big bear of a man, almost as ugly as I am."

She smiled dutifully at the sally. She could think of a whole slew of adjectives to describe Cutter Smith. *Ugly* wasn't one of them.

Scarred, yes. *Rough around the edges*, definitely. Yet capable of such incredible tenderness that Mallory's heart ached with the memory of it. Wrenching her gaze from his profile, she let it drop to the filigree band on her finger.

"Mike will be wearing a windbreaker with the

insignia of the Military Marksmanship Association on the pocket. Rifles crossed over a bull's-eye." He shot her a quick look. "Got that?"

"Rifles crossed over a bull's-eye. Got it."

The short-term parking garage was jammed, but Cutter lucked out and found a slot only a few yards from the second-story walkway to the departure terminal.

He carried the tote, Mallory the brightly colored shopping bag. She couldn't believe she'd crossed this same walkway less than a week ago, blithely unaware she was being stalked by the man at her side. Her little burst of resentment quickly fizzled. Too much had happened, and her feelings for Cutter were too confused, to work up much of a mad at this point.

The replacement passport was waiting at the Delta Business Class desk, as promised, along with a revised return ticket.

"We bumped you up to Business Class," the helpful clerk advised after issuing a boarding pass. "Do you have any luggage to check?"

With a strangled laugh, Mallory shook her head. "Not this time."

"Very well. Your aircraft will begin boarding at Gate 42B in approximately one hour. Have a good flight home, Mademoiselle Dawes."

"Was Business Class your doing?" she asked as Cutter took her arm to weave a path through the throngs of travelers toward the shops at the end of the concourse. The distinctive blue-and-white sign above the American Express kiosk stood out like a beacon.

"I figured you deserved at least that much of a break after..."

He broke off, his grip tightening. When his eyes narrowed on something beyond her, Mallory twisted around to see what had snared his attention. Shock rippled through her as she spotted her face staring back at her from the giant TV screen mounted above the heads of the travelers.

There she was, backdropped against the stark, modernistic portrait in Madame d'Marchand's library. Same shoulder-length blond bob. Same wary brown eyes. Same navy blazer. The commentary was in French and muffled by the noise in the terminal but Mallory got the gist of it when the screen split to display Congressman Kent's image alongside hers. A moment later, both were replaced by a mug shot of Remy Duchette.

"Didn't take long for them to get the footage on-air," she commented, her throat tight.

"That was the idea," Cutter reminded her. "The story's probably been running every half hour since the interview."

"Hold this a moment, would you?"

Passing him the shopping bag, she fumbled in her purse for her sunglasses. She hadn't hidden behind them in days. Something inside her died a little at having to resort to their shield again.

The clerk in the American Express kiosk responded with the same efficiency as the airline representative. It was obvious he'd seen the news flash. Curiosity prompted several sidelong glances, but he refrained from comment except to request Mallory's signature in several places. She walked out of the kiosk fifteen minutes later with money in her purse for the first time since the day she'd arrived.

"Wonder what happened to the flag on my accounts?" she drawled while she and Cutter once again threaded through the crowds.

"Beats me."

His totally fake innocence scored a huff from Mallory. A moment later, she bumped to a stop.

"Look."

Her pointing finger drew his attention to a display of plastic snow globes in the window of a souvenir shop. Amid the bubble-encased Eiffel Towers and Arc de Triomphes was the cathedral of Mont St. Michel, rising from a blue plastic sea.

"I *have* to get one of those."

She found a boxed globe easily enough, but the long line at the register moved at a snail's pace. The business with American Express had eaten a chunk out of her hour prior to boarding. The long lines at security would devour the rest. Disappointed, Mallory put the globe back on the shelf.

"I'll pick one up after I see you aboard the plane,"

Cutter promised. "Do you need to make a pit stop before we hit security?"

"I'm okay."

She assumed they'd say goodbye at the security checkpoint, since only ticketed passengers were allowed beyond. Cutter, evidently, had other plans.

When they approached the checkpoint, he produced an ID and an official-looking document and pulled one of the security inspectors aside. That worthy individual skimmed the paperwork, pursed his lips and gestured to a fellow officer. Mallory caught only snatches of the intense conversations that ensued, but picked up several references to Interpol. Cutter finally broke away and strode back to her.

"Seems to be a problem here with my permit to carry concealed," he said, his voice low and for her ears only.

"You're armed?"

His hooked brow made her realize how stupid that sounded. Of course, he had his gun strapped to his ankle. This was his job. *She* was his job.

"I need to talk to the director of security," Cutter told her. "Wait for me here. Right here."

"It's getting close to boarding time."

"I'll square this away as quickly as I can. If I'm not back in ten minutes, go on through. I'll meet you at the gate. If they call your flight, get on board. You know what to do when you deplane."

She covered her sudden, sinking sensation with a brisk nod. "Look for Mike Callahan. Big. Ugly. Crossed rifles. Bull's-eye."

"Be sure to tell him about the ugly part."

"I will."

"Just in case, you'd better take this with you."

She assumed he was referring to the tote he'd carried through the terminal with her. Before she could reach for it, however, he wrapped his hands around her upper arms and pulled her forward for a long, hard kiss.

"Wait here," he growled, when he released her. "Ten minutes."

Cutter stalked back to the two security officials, torn between the need to get Mallory on that plane and the equally fierce need to keep her in his sight until she was aboard.

It took one call to Interpol and another to OMEGA to untangle the confusion over the permit. By Cutter's watch, he was back at the security checkpoint in nine and a half minutes. His brows slashing together, he skimmed the entire vicinity. Mallory wasn't anywhere in sight.

Spotting the official who'd stopped him in languid conversation with another employee, he thrust through the crowd. "The woman I was with," he bit out. "The blonde. Did she pass through security?"

"No, monsieur. She waits for you, then goes back to the concourse."

"Dammit!"

If Mallory had decided to use the delay to buy that snow globe, Cutter would rip her a new one.

"She comes back soon," the inspector added helpfully. "I hear her tell her friend she has not much time."

"What friend?"

"The woman who greets her. She carries a shopping bag, too. The same as mademoiselle's."

Cutter whirled, his mind racing. Who the hell had Mallory hooked up with? A fellow shoe addict? A representative of Yvette d'Marchand, bearing more gifts? Yvette herself, driven by curiosity about the houseguest who'd generated such a spate of publicity?

Or someone else? Someone who'd tried to use Mallory's connection to d'Marchand once before to get to her?

His stomach clenching, Cutter barged around clumps of travelers and swept through the gift shop on the run. Customers scattered. The clerk at the register shouted a protest. A string of muttered curses followed him out again.

His heart jackhammered against his ribs when he burst onto the cavernous concourse and skidded to a stop. He spun left, searching the crowd, praying for a glimpse of Mallory's navy blazer or pale gold hair.

He swung to the right and had started for the Delta

reservation counter when he spotted her through the glass windows. She was on the walkway leading to the parking garage, arm-in-arm with a slender brunette in designer jeans and a mink vest. They moved at a good clip but both, he saw with a jolt of disbelief, were laughing.

Cutter's step slowed. Ice coated his veins. The noisy terminal faded, replaced in his frozen mind by a dark, silent munitions warehouse.

Eva had left an urgent message for Cutter to meet her there. Said she'd put the squeeze on one of her sources and learned that the stolen munitions they'd been tracking were in a crate hidden inside the warehouse. He'd slipped over the wall an hour early, intending to reconnoiter. A half dozen yards from the entrance to the warehouse he'd picked up the murmur of voices…accompanied by the unmistakable timbre of Eva's low, rippling laugh. Then a truck had rumbled up, the warehouse doors opened and she'd walked into the spear of headlights.

Cutter never knew which of them fired the shot that ignited the munitions stored inside the warehouse. He wasn't even sure she'd screamed his name before the explosion knocked him on his ass and the flames consumed him.

Now, with the echo of her laughter ringing in his ears, the agony of those months in the burn ward gripped Cutter like a vise. Needles of pain seemed to shoot through his jaw and neck. He couldn't breathe, couldn't move, couldn't force any thought through his frozen mind except one. Mallory was walking away from him. Arm in arm with a stranger. Laughing.

"Keep walking."

The woman in the mink vest reinforced the soft command by digging her gun in deeper.

"I'm telling you the truth," Mallory said desperately. "I don't have the damned disk."

"So you wish me to believe." The brunette's smile belied the menace in her eyes. "I saw your performance on TV. It was worthy of the Bolshoi. How fortunate that I was in Paris and could intercept you at the airport."

Her English was as flawless as her face, but the reference to the Bolshoi generated the sickening suspicion that she worked for the nameless, faceless Russian Cutter was after.

"I wasn't performing! I *did* lose my suitcase to the riptide at Mont St. Michel. I *am* going home."

"You've caused me considerable inconvenience, Ms. Dawes. Please don't try my patience further. Walk." The gun gouged into her ribs. "And smile for these nice people."

Mallory stretched her lips at the travelers hurrying in the opposite direction, but inside she screamed with frustration and fear and a fast-growing fury.

She'd been standing less than a half dozen yards from the security checkpoint when this svelte brunette had sauntered by. Catching sight of the gold-embossed shopping bag, the woman held up a similar one of her own and strolled over. To talk shoes, Mallory assumed. The next thing she knew, she had a gun sticking in her side and was being hustled toward the exit.

She could guess what Cutter would think when he discovered she'd skipped. He'd believe she knew about the disk all along, that she grabbed this opportunity to escape.

The brunette must have been reading her mind. "This man you were with. The one you kissed. Does he know about the disk?"

She was damned if she'd tell the woman anything. "No."

"So it is just you and your Congressman Kent who make this deal?"

"Kent?" Mallory stumbled, numb with shock. "Are you saying *Kent* burned that data to disk?"

"Do you think you're the only woman he pawed?" Amusement laced the reply. "He is a pig, that one, and easily led by his dick. And now he pays dearly for his pleasure." Satisfaction thrummed through her voice. "The data he pulled off your computer is worth millions. My best haul to date."

Reeling, Mallory realized she wasn't dealing

with an underling. This was the big kahuna. Struggling to overcome her shock, she swiped her tongue over dry lips.

"How…? How did Kent get the disk into my suitcase?"

"I neither know nor care. You'll have to ask him when next you see him."

Yeah, right.

The woman's mocking reply more than convinced Mallory she wouldn't live to put the question to Kent—or to tip authorities to the fact that the shadowy figure they'd labeled the Russian was a woman. It also fueled her simmering fury into a fast, furious boil.

Enough was enough! She'd been groped by a man she'd admired. Seen her allegations of sexual harassment turned against her. Endured the humiliation of being publicly branded a whore. Been tailed across France by an undercover agent. She was *damned* if she'd let this bitch hustle her into a car at gunpoint.

Digging in her heels, she dragged the woman to an abrupt halt. "I'm not going anywhere with you."

"Yes, you are." The gun barrel bruised her ribs. "Keep walking, Ms. Dawes."

"No."

"Don't make me hurt you. Walk."

Mallory's reply was to twist violently. At the same instant she let swing with the shopping bag gripped in her free hand. The shoebox whipped across her body in a vicious arc and smacked the brunette square in the face.

The woman stumbled, recovered, whirled, caught the thud of pounding feet. Mallory heard it, too. Her heart stuttering, she saw the Russian's gun jerk a few inches to the left.

Cutter! That had to be Cutter the woman had in her sights!

Terror leaping through her veins, Mallory put every ounce of strength she possessed into another swing.

Chapter 15

Mike Callahan was waiting when Mallory and Cutter deplaned at Dulles an exhausting thirty-six hours later.

They'd spent most of those hours holed up at Interpol. While Mallory watched through a one-way mirror, Cutter and several very skilled interrogators grilled the woman they soon identified as Catherine Halston, aka Fatima Allende, aka Irina Petrov.

Cool and unruffled, Petrov had admitted to a half dozen other aliases. In exchange for the promise of a reduced sentence, she also offered to provide video of her afternoon trysts with Ashton Kent in a posh D.C. hotel—including segments detailing his reluctant agreement to provide identity data as the price for keeping silent about his illicit liaison.

After the session at Interpol, Mallory had contrived a quick visit to Yvette d'Marchand's Paris boutique to thank the designer in person for the shoes now adorning her feet. Brilliant aquamarine crystals studded the thick wedge soles and decorated the straps that crisscrossed over her feet, wrapped around her ankles, and tied midway up her calf.

The glittering three-inch platforms gave her the necessary boost to meet Mike Callahan eye to eye. Almost. He was as tall and tough-looking as Cutter had indicated, but nowhere near as ugly. When she told him so, he shot his fellow agent a dry look.

"Thanks, Slash."

"I calls 'em as I sees 'em, Hawk."

Cutter used the drive in from Dulles to provide an update on the results of the interrogation. Callahan, in turn, shared the dossier he'd compiled on each of the Russian's various aliases.

"The woman got around. Remember the op that came apart on us in Hong Kong?"

Cutter let out a low whistle. "That was her?"

"That was her."

The thick file Callahan passed over his shoulder prompted a question from Mallory.

"Do you have a copy of the dossier you compiled on me?"

"I don't know." He glanced in the rearview mirror. "Do I?"

"You might as well show her," Cutter said. "I've already taken a ration of grief over it."

Mallory had to admit this OMEGA gang was nothing if not thorough. The file she thumbed through contained everything from her taste in music to her preference for cookie dough and chocolate chip ice cream, as extracted from records of her credit card purchases. She was still poring through the file when they drove into an underground parking garage.

Fifteen minutes later, Cutter and his partner whisked her onto an elevator that appeared out of nowhere. After a short, swift ride, it opened in an elegant anteroom. The woman who rose and came around her desk to greet them had coal-black hair, blue eyes and a smile that lit up the room.

"It's a pleasure to meet you, Ms. Dawes. I'm Gillian Ridgeway, filling in as executive assistant to the Special Envoy. He's expecting you. Before I buzz you in, I have to know…"

Her eager gaze dropped to Mallory's feet.

"Are those the Yvette d'Marchand's? The ones you used to deck the Russian?"

"They are."

Hiking up her jeans, Mallory displayed the lethal weapons. The aquamarine crystals caught the slanting sunbeam and threw it back in a zillion points of light.

"Oooh! I want a pair of those."

"There was a catalog in the box. They come in every color. You should get sapphire, to match your eyes."

Mike Callahan made an inarticulate sound that could have been a grunt or a mere clearing of his throat. Whatever it was, the small noise recalled the woman to her duties.

"I'll tell Uncle Nick you're here. Mac is with him, by the way."

Escorted by Cutter and Mike, Mallory entered a sunlit office redolent with the scent of polished mahogany and well-soaped leather. When the President's Special Envoy came from behind his desk, she felt her brows soar. Cutter had warned her to expect smooth and sophisticated. He'd left out the drop-dead gorgeous part.

Nick Jensen was as tall as his two operatives, but the similarities stopped there. Cutter and Mike were both dark-haired and more rugged than handsome. With his tanned skin, blue eyes and tawny hair, Jensen looked like an older and more polished Brad Pitt.

"Sorry we put you through the wringer in Normandy," he said with a smile Mallory suspected had raised goose bumps on more females than he could count. "I hope you understand the necessity."

"I do now. If you'd asked me a few days ago, I might not be so ready to forgive or forget."

"The situation got a little rougher than expected."

"It always does."

That came from a long-legged brunette in a severely tailored gray pantsuit with a gigantic pink peony pinned to the lapel. Pushing off her perch on the conference table, she came forward. Lightning made the introductions.

"This is my wife, Mackenzie Blair-Jensen. She was working some communications issues upstairs when Hawk—Mike—called to say you were en route, and she decided to hang around."

The vivacious brunette took Mallory's hand in a firm, no-nonsense grip. "I *had* to meet the woman who took down an international thug with a thousand-dollar pair of shoes. Way to go, Ms. Dawes."

Her glance, too, zinged south.

"Is that them?"

"It is."

An obliging Mallory once again showed off her trophies. The sparkling platforms infected the other woman with instant greed.

"Guess what I want for Christmas, husband of mine."

"Duly noted. Now if you ladies don't mind, we should talk business instead of shoes."

The mood in the sunny office immediately sobered. Suggesting everyone take a seat at the mahogany conference table, Nick Jensen laid out his plan of attack.

"I've set up an appointment with Congressman Kent a little more than an hour from now. Cutter and Mike will accompany me. Kent thinks I want to discuss the President's new counter-terrorism initiative. He *isn't* expecting me to show up with you two. Or with the House of Representatives Master at Arms, two detectives and a U.S. district attorney."

That should get Kent's attention, Mallory thought with unrestrained glee.

"We'll show him the airport surveillance tapes," Jensen continued, "and ask if he recognizes the woman accompanying Ms. Dawes. Only then will we produce sworn statements by Irina Petrov."

Jensen's glance swept the table.

"That's when we ask him what he knows about the disk containing the stolen data pulled off a computer in his office."

Mallory saw only one problem with the proposed plan and voiced it in no uncertain terms. "I want to be present when you do."

"We've discussed that," Cutter said evenly.

They had, she acknowledged with a curt nod. In Paris and on the long flight home. His argument that Mallory's presence would alert the reporters who prowled the halls of Congress held weight. Just not enough to convince her to sit on her hands while they confronted the man who'd made her life a living hell.

"I'll wear a disguise if necessary, but I want to see Kent's face when you tell him about the video tapes."

"Mallory…"

"I'm with Ms. Dawes." The support came from Mackenzie Blair-Jensen. "She's earned the right to be in at the kill. Plus she'll add to the shock value when Kent sees her."

Lightning drummed his fingers on the conference table and deferred to his field agent. "It's your call, Slash."

"No," Mallory countered swiftly, "it isn't. I didn't ask to be part of this operation, but now that I am, I want to see it through to the end. Correction, I *intend* to see it through to the end."

The men exchanged glances. Even Mackenzie looked surprised. Mallory suspected few people stood up to Lightning, but she refused to cave. Jaw set, she folded her arms and matched Cutter glower for glower.

"Okay," he conceded. "You're in. On one condition. We still don't know how that disk got in your suitcase. We're guessing Kent used an agent. We're also guessing that was his chief of staff, Dillon Porter. We don't *think* either of them will try to resist or turn violent when confronted, but we can't rule out the possibility. You take your cues from me. If the situation looks like it might deteriorate, you do what I say, when I say. Understood?"

"Yes, *sir!*"

A look of amusement crept into Jensen's eyes as they shifted to his wife. "She sounds a lot like someone else I know."

"I can't imagine who." With a flip of her hair, Mackenzie shoved away from the table. "Come with me, Ms. Dawes. I'll take you upstairs while the boys work out the final details. Give our wizards in Field Dress fifteen minutes and your own mother won't recognize you."

The vivacious brunette whisked Mallory out of the office. The door had barely shut behind them, however, before she pounced.

"Okay, the shoes are fantastic, but I want the real story on that ring."

"So do I." Abandoning her desk, the dark-haired executive assistant joined Mackenzie to ogle the diamonds and white gold.

"We saw the news conference," she confided. "We couldn't wait to meet the woman who brought Slash to his knees."

"Cutter was just performing for the cameras."

Mackenzie gave a snort. Gillian sniggered.

"Do you know how Slash got those scars?" the older woman asked.

"He said it was an explosion."

"Did he say who ignited it?"

"No."

"Make him tell you sometime. Until then, take my word for it. Cutter Smith wouldn't put a ring on *any* woman's finger unless he meant for it to stay there."

After that startling disclosure, the confrontation in Ashton Kent's office proved something of an anticlimax.

Mallory's auburn wig and subtly altered features got her past the palace guard without so much as a flicker of recognition. Even Dillon Porter gaped when Nick Jensen identified her along with the two detectives and U.S. district attorney. Congressman Kent blustered, protesting her presence, until Jensen cut him off at the knees.

After that, matters moved at warp speed. Mike Callahan and one of the detectives led a protesting Porter into another room. The second detective advised Congressman Kent of his rights. Each thinking the other had ratted on him, Kent and Porter soon admitted to a conspiracy to cover up the congressman's illicit affairs and use Mallory as a mule to deliver the blackmail payoff. Less than an hour after entering her old office, Mallory watched as her former boss was handcuffed and led out.

Someone had alerted the media. They'd assembled in droves and forced Kent to run a brutal gauntlet. Still in disguise, Mallory stood off to the side. She experienced none of the euphoria she'd expected at seeing the once-mighty legislator brought low.

"You okay?"

Sighing, she turned to Cutter. "I thought this would make up for some of the humiliation and hurt."

"Didn't it?"

"No. It just made me feel…sad."

They stood side by side until the circus trailed down the steps of the Capitol.

"I was thinking…"

Cutter hesitated, sounding unsure of himself for the first time that Mallory could remember.

"You were thinking…?" she prompted.

"I got back from Central America and hopped on a plane right for France. Barely had time to shave between flights."

He scraped a hand over his jaw, as if feeling for the whiskers he'd grown in the jungle.

"The thing is, I've racked up more vacation time than I know what to do with. I thought maybe you might want to go back to France, finish that trip you planned in such meticulous detail."

"When?" she asked, her heart starting to pound.

"I'm ready whenever you are."

They'd crawled off a plane less than four hours ago. Mallory hadn't slept in longer than she could recall. She knew darn well her skin sagged like an old sponge under the makeup OMEGA's Field Dress Unit had so skillfully applied. Yet joy sang through her as she framed Cutter's bristly cheeks between her palms.

"Let's go now. Right this minute."

Epilogue

Mallory stood at the window of the small pension. Moonlight washed over her. A cold, damp breeze blew in through the open panes. Hugging her arms for warmth, she filled her lungs with the sharp sea air.

Instead of following the itinerary Mallory had planned originally in such meticulous detail, she and Cutter had holed up in this tiny hotel carved out of the ancient walls. The pension wasn't as grand as Yvette d'Marchand's château or anywhere near as modern. Cutter had lugged their hastily packed bags up three flights of stairs, grumbling with every step over the lack of modern conveniences like elevators and man-sized showers. His good-natured complaints had died when he'd taken in the view from their balcony window, however.

Mallory drank it in now, her spirits soaring. Floodlights illuminated the tall spire topped by the gilded statue of St. Michael slaying his dragon. Below and beyond, the moon-washed waters of the Gulf of St. Malo stretched as far as she could see.

"The tide's in," Cutter commented.

"So it is."

Padding across the bedroom on bare feet, he slid his arms around her waist. Her head drifted back against his shoulder.

They and the other inhabitants of St. Michel were completely cut off from the rest of the world. Just the way they wanted it.

"Wonder if any cars or buses washed away?" she mused.

"Probably." A chuckle rumbled up from his chest. "With any luck, ours was one of them."

Then he bent to nuzzle her neck and Mallory forgot the tide, forgot the view, forgot everything but the sizzle he ignited just under her skin. Alternating kisses with stinging little nips, he fanned the sparks to a five-alarm blaze.

"Have I mentioned that I love you?" he muttered between bites.

"Not in the last hour or so."

"I do, you know."

"I know. Same goes." Twisting around in his arms, she kissed the underside of his chin. The tough, puckered skin tugged at her heart. "Mackenzie said I should ask you who ignited the explosion that caused these. I got the impression it was a woman."

"It was." His palms cupped her face. "She's history, sweetheart, and not worth wasting this moonlight on."

He was right. The present was too full, and the future held no room for shadows from the past. Taking his hand in hers, Mallory led him back to bed.

* * * * *

Silhouette® Romantic Suspense
keeps getting hotter!
Turn the page for a sneak preview
of Wendy Rosnau's latest SPY GAMES *title,*
SLEEPING WITH DANGER

Available November 2007

Silhouette® Romantic Suspense—
Sparked by Danger, Fueled by Passion!

Melita had been expecting a chaste quick kiss of the generic variety. But this kiss with Sully was the kind that sparked a dying flame to life. The kind of kiss you can't plan for. The kind of kiss memories are built on.

The memory of her murdered lover, Nemo, came to her then and she made a starved little noise in the back of her throat. She raised her arms and threaded her fingers through Sully's hair, pulled him closer. Felt his body settle, then melt into her.

In that instant her hunger for him grew, and his for her. She pressed herself to him with more urgency, and he responded in kind.

Melita came out of her kiss-induced memory of Nemo with a start. "Wait a minute." She pushed Sully away from her. "You bastard!"

She spit two nasty words at him in Greek, then wiped his kiss from her lips.

"I thought you deserved some solid proof that I'm still in one piece." He started for the door. "The clock's ticking, honey. Come on, let's get out of here."

"That's it? You sucker me into kissing you, and that's all you have to say?"

"I'm sorry. How's that?"

He didn't sound sorry in the least. "You're—"

"Getting out of this godforsaken prison cell. Stop whining and let's go."

"Not if I was being shot at sunrise. Go. You deserve whatever you get if you walk out that door."

He turned back. "Freedom is what I'm going to get."

"A second of freedom before the guards in the hall shoot you." She jammed her hands on her hips. "And to think I was worried about you."

"If you're staying behind, it's no skin off my ass."

"Wait! What about our deal?"

"You just said you're not coming. Make up your mind."

"Have you forgotten we need a boat?"

"How could I? You keep harping on it."

"I'm not going without a boat. And those guards

out there aren't going to just let you walk out of here. You need me and we need a plan."

"I already have a plan. I'm getting out of here. That's the plan."

"I should have realized that you never intended to take me with you from the very beginning. You're a liar and a coward."

Of everything she had read, there was nothing in Sully Paxton's file that hinted he was a coward, but it was the one word that seemed to register in that one-track mind of his. The look he nailed her with a second later was pure venom.

He came at her so quickly she didn't have time to get out of his way. "You know I'm not a coward."

"Prove it. Give me until dawn. I need one more night to put everything in place before we leave the island."

"You're asking me to stay in this cell one more night…and trust you?"

"Yes."

He snorted. "Yesterday you knew they were planning to harm me, but instead of doing something about it you went to bed and never gave me a second thought. Suppose tonight you do the same. By tomorrow I might damned well be in my grave."

"Okay, I screwed up. I won't do it again." Melita sucked in a ragged breath. "I can't leave this minute. Dawn, Sully. Wait until dawn." When he looked as if he was about to say no, she pleaded, "Please wait for me."

"You're asking a lot. The door's open now. I would be a fool to hang around here and trust that you'll be back."

"What you can trust is that I want off this island as badly as you do, and you're my only hope."

"I must be crazy."

"Is that a yes?"

"Dammit!" He turned his back on her. Swore twice more.

"You won't be sorry."

He turned around. "I already am. How about we seal this new deal?"

He was staring at her lips. Suddenly Melita knew what he expected. "We already sealed it."

"One more. You enjoyed it. Admit it."

"I enjoyed it because I was kissing someone else."

He laughed. "That's a good one."

"It's true. It might have been your lips, but it wasn't you I was kissing."

"If that's your excuse for wanting to kiss me, then—"

"I was kissing Nemo."

"What's a nemo?"

Melita gave Sully a look that clearly told him that he was trespassing on sacred ground. She was about to enforce it with a warning when a voice in the hall jerked them both to attention.

She bolted away from the wall. "Get back in bed. Hurry. I'll be here before dawn."

She didn't reach the door before he snagged her arm, pulled her up against him and planted a kiss on her lips that took her completely by surprise.

When he released her, he said, "If you're confused about who just kissed you, the name's Sully. I'll be here waiting at dawn. Don't be late."

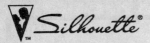

Romantic
SUSPENSE

**Sparked by Danger,
Fueled by Passion.**

Onyxx agent Sully Paxton's only chance of
survival lies in the hands of his enemy's daughter
Melita Krizova. He doesn't know he's a pawn in the
beautiful island girl's own plan for escape. Can
they survive their ruses and their fiery attraction?

*Look for the next installment in the
Spy Games miniseries,*

*Sleeping with
Danger*
by Wendy Rosnau

Available November 2007 wherever you buy books.

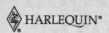

REQUEST YOUR
FREE BOOKS!

2 FREE NOVELS PLUS 2 FREE GIFTS!

Silhouette® Romantic

SUSPENSE

Sparked by Danger, Fueled by Passion!

YES! Please send me 2 FREE Silhouette® Romantic Suspense novels and my 2 FREE gifts. After receiving them, if I don't wish to receive any more books, I can return the shipping statement marked "cancel." If I don't cancel, I will receive 4 brand-new novels every month and be billed just $4.24 per book in the U.S., or $4.99 per book in Canada, plus 25¢ shipping and handling per book plus applicable taxes, if any*. That's a savings of at least 15% off the cover price! I understand that accepting the 2 free books and gifts places me under no obligation to buy anything. I can always return a shipment and cancel at any time. Even if I never buy another book from Silhouette, the two free books and gifts are mine to keep forever.

240 SDN EEX6   340 SDN EEYJ

Name	(PLEASE PRINT)	
Address		Apt. #
City	State/Prov.	Zip/Postal Code

Signature (if under 18, a parent or guardian must sign)

Mail to the **Silhouette Reader Service**™:
IN U.S.A.: P.O. Box 1867, Buffalo, NY 14240-1867
IN CANADA: P.O. Box 609, Fort Erie, Ontario L2A 5X3

Not valid to current Silhouette Intimate Moments subscribers.

Want to try two free books from another line?
Call 1-800-873-8635 or visit www.morefreebooks.com.

* Terms and prices subject to change without notice. NY residents add applicable sales tax. Canadian residents will be charged applicable provincial taxes and GST. This offer is limited to one order per household. All orders subject to approval. Credit or debit balances in a customer's account(s) may be offset by any other outstanding balance owed by or to the customer. Please allow 4 to 6 weeks for delivery.

Your Privacy: Silhouette is committed to protecting your privacy. Our Privacy Policy is available online at www.eHarlequin.com or upon request from the Reader Service. From time to time we make our lists of customers available to reputable firms who may have a product or service of interest to you. If you would prefer we not share your name and address, please check here. ☐

SRS07

HARLEQUIN® Romance®

New York Times bestselling author

DIANA PALMER

Handsome, eligible ranch owner Stuart York knew
Ivy Conley was too young for him, so he closed his heart
to her and sent her away—despite the fireworks between
them. Now, years later, Ivy is determined not to be
treated like a little girl anymore…but for some reason,
Stuart is always fighting her battles for her. And safe in
Stuart's arms makes Ivy feel like a woman…his woman.

Winter Roses

Available November.

HRIBC03985

Silhouette®

Romantic

SUSPENSE

COMING NEXT MONTH

**#1487 HOLIDAY HEROES—"The Best Noel" by Rachel Lee,
"Christmas at His Command" by Catherine Mann**
Jump into the holiday season with two military-themed short stories
by *New York Times* bestselling author Rachel Lee and RITA® Award-
winning author Catherine Mann.

#1488 KISS OR KILL—Lyn Stone
Mission: Impassioned
When undercover agent Renee Leblanc recognizes Lazlo operative
Mark Alexander at a secret meeting, she fears her alias will be blown.
Mark realizes Renee is following the same lead and proposes they
partner up...but their passion for one another could be deadly.

#1489 SLEEPING WITH DANGER—Wendy Rosnau
Spy Games
Onyxx agent Sully Paxton's only chance of survival lies in the hands of
his enemy's daughter, Melita Krizova. He doesn't know he's a pawn in
the beautiful island girl's own plan for escape. Can they survive each
other's ruses and their fiery attraction?

#1490 SEDUCING THE MERCENARY—Loreth Anne White
Shadow Soldiers
To the rest of the world, Jean-Charles Laroque is a dangerous tyrant.
But Dr. Emily Carlin gains access to his true identity and in doing
so becomes a captive in his game of deception and betrayal—all the
while falling under the mercenary's seductive spell.

SRSCNM1007